London Hospital Midwives

Delivering miracles and meeting their match!

In Queen Victoria Hospital's maternity wing, midwives and friends Esther, Carly, Chloe and Izzy deliver miracles every day—but haven't found their own happily-ever-afters!

All that's about to change when some unexpected arrivals of the tall, dedicated and handsome kind shake up the maternity ward and the lives— and hearts—of these amazing midwives!

Cinderella and the Surgeon by Scarlet Wilson
Miracle Baby for the Midwife by Tina Beckett

Both available now!

Reunited by Their Secret Daughter by Emily Forbes
A Fling to Steal Her Heart by Sue MacKay

Coming next month!

But now Esther knew.

Now she knew why he acted that way. And she had understood. He had to learn to trust his colleagues, her included.

He looked at her again and she could sense the change in atmosphere from them both. They'd both revealed a tiny part of themselves. Like Harry, she didn't want him to feel sorry for her, but now at least they understood each other's reasons—his, for being pedantic about instructions, and hers, for wanting to work so hard.

If she lit a match in here right now she was sure the place would go up in flames.

She licked her lips. His eyes were watching her every move, and she could feel the tiny little hairs on her body standing to attention underneath the thick robe.

If he just took a few steps forward…

She blinked and breathed in. She was being ridiculous. She knew she was. But the prickles on her skin told her differently. And the way that Harry was looking at her…

CINDERELLA
AND THE SURGEON

———

SCARLET WILSON

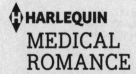

HARLEQUIN

MEDICAL
ROMANCE

HARLEQUIN®
MEDICAL
ROMANCE™

Recycling programs
for this product may
not exist in your area.

ISBN-13: 978-1-335-14919-0

Cinderella and the Surgeon

Copyright © 2020 by Scarlet Wilson

All rights reserved. No part of this book may be used or reproduced in any manner whatsoever without written permission except in the case of brief quotations embodied in critical articles and reviews.

This is a work of fiction. Names, characters, places and incidents are either the product of the author's imagination or are used fictitiously. Any resemblance to actual persons, living or dead, businesses, companies, events or locales is entirely coincidental.

This edition published by arrangement with Harlequin Books S.A.

For questions and comments about the quality of this book, please contact us at CustomerService@Harlequin.com.

Harlequin Enterprises ULC
22 Adelaide St. West, 40th Floor
Toronto, Ontario M5H 4E3, Canada
www.Harlequin.com

Printed in U.S.A.

Visit the Author Profile page
at Harlequin.com for more titles.

This book is dedicated to my lifelong friend
Julie Clark. When she reads it,
she will understand why!

And to my fabulous editor Carly Byrne for giving me
a helping hand when I needed it most.

CHAPTER ONE

ESTHER MCDONALD RUBBED her eyes for the twentieth time as she made her way to work. She'd hoped the walk along the footpath next to the Thames would have woken her up a little, but it clearly wasn't working.

She'd pulled an extra shift last night working until midnight at another hospital in London. Anything to help pull in some extra cash. She already planned to text the agency again today to see if they had anything else for her.

It wasn't that her own job wasn't well paid. It was and she loved working in the neonatal ICU at the Queen Victoria. But right now she needed every penny she could get. So that meant working every shift available.

She was lucky. Because she was dual-trained she could work as a nurse or a midwife, which meant she had multiple opportunities for extra shifts. Usually she could pick up shifts at short notice for the A&E department in the Queen

Victoria on her scheduled days off. But the duty manager had noticed how often she'd been working and had passed comment more than once. So, Esther had registered with an agency as well.

She filed through the main doors of the hospital along with a whole host of other staff heading for the early shift. She was worried about a tiny preemie she'd been looking after for the last few days in ICU. Billy, the twenty-four-weeker with a heart defect, had seemed even more fragile than normal yesterday afternoon when she'd left. His young mother hadn't left his side since he'd been born a few days earlier and was looking sicker and sicker herself. Esther just hoped the 'wonder' doc they'd all been talking about had finally managed to turn up to assess the little guy. Billy needed surgery that only a few neonatal cardiac surgeons could do. Trouble was, this guy had been over in France operating on another baby, so Billy had been left waiting.

She tugged her pale blue scrubs over her head and pulled her hair back into a ponytail, catching a quick glance of herself in the changing room mirror. Ugh. She looked awful. The quick sweep of make-up she'd stuck on her face this morning couldn't hide the dark circles under her eyes.

As she headed to the stairs her stomach grumbled loudly. She'd been so tired she hadn't had time to make breakfast this morning. She'd have to try and sweet-talk her colleagues into letting her take first break. One of the Queen Victoria's freshly baked scones would easily fill the huge gap in her stomach. She smiled at the thought of it.

'Morning,' she said in her best bright voice as she entered the NICU, stowing her bag and washing her hands. She got a little buzz every time she walked through the door. It was everything, the lighting, the sounds, the staff and patients—even the smell. She'd done her nurse training in Edinburgh and came down to London to also complete her midwifery training. Only a few specialist centres offered the shortened eighteen-month training these days and she'd been delighted to join the programme at the Queen Victoria, joining in with an already partly trained direct entry midwifery programme. She'd made some of the best friends she'd ever had—and even though some of them had gone to other parts of the world now, they were all still in touch.

The midwifery training had been a revelation for her. Esther had always imagined she'd end up as a community midwife, but from the first second she'd set foot in the NICU, she'd known that's where her heart lay. There was something about the vulnerability of these tiny babies. The role of often being their safe-guarder in the first few days of their lives. The little bits of progress she could see every day.

Of course, there could often be heartbreak. Her job was as much to take care of the families as it was to take care of the babies. But there was something so special about helping a preterm baby latch on to their mother for the first time. Or watching them become more aware of the world around them. Or seeing their reactions to lights or voices. Now she was here, she couldn't imagine working any place else.

One of the other midwives stood up and put her bag over her shoulder.

Esther glanced at the chart. 'How's Billy doing?' She checked the whiteboard, making sure she'd been assigned her favourite patient again today. Yip. Perfect. Billy, and a thirty-six-weeker in the next crib who'd been born to a diabetic mother in the early hours of the morning. That little one was likely just being monitored for a few hours to keep an eye on blood sugars.

Ruth, the other midwife, sighed. 'You look tired.'

'I am. Weird. Extra shifts never usually bother me.' Esther stretched out her back. 'You know how things are. Win the lottery and give me a share and I promise I won't work an extra shift again. Until then, I'll take all I can get.'

Ruth shot her a look and started the handover.

'Billy hasn't had a good night. His sats dropped, his feeding tube dislodged and X-ray haven't been able to get back up to ensure the new one is in the correct place. Hence, his feeds haven't started again.'

Esther shook her head. She knew exactly how important it was to ensure the nasogastric feeding tube had gone into the stomach and not a baby's lungs. No feeding could commence until it was confirmed.

'I'll call them again. If Callum's working I'm sure he can get someone up here now.'

Ruth smiled. 'Perfect. He always listens to you.'

She scanned the rest of the charts. 'Anything else?'

Ruth nodded. 'Billy's cardiac surgeon is supposed to arrive today. No idea when, but all his tests have been completed, so hopefully the surgeon will just be able to check them all, listen to his chest and schedule the surgery.'

Esther nodded. *Please let it be today.*

'By the way,' said Ruth as she handed Esther another chart. 'He's supposed to be a duke or something.'

Esther had already started scanning the other chart. The other baby was Laura, thirty-six weeks, born via emergency caesarean section to a Type 1 diabetic mother. Laura's blood sugar levels had been erratic for a few hours after delivery. That could happen with babies born to diabetic mothers, and it wasn't unusual for a baby to have close monitoring for just a few hours. Laura's levels had stabilised in the last hour, so Esther would just do a few more checks, then get her back to her mother's bedside.

She looked up and wrinkled her nose. 'What did you just say?'

Ruth laughed. 'I said the new surgeon. He's a prince or a duke or something.'

Esther shrugged. 'And what difference does that make? Is that why he's late? He's too busy with his—' she held up her fingers '—other duties.' She frowned as she picked up some nearby equipment. 'Better not be why he's keeping my baby waiting.'

Ruth shook her head as she picked up her bag to leave. 'Lighten up. Maybe this new guy is single.' Ruth sighed and gave Esther a look that made her want to run a million miles away. Pity. Esther hated that. She hated anyone feeling sorry for the poor little Scots girl. 'All I'm saying is that maybe there's more to life than work, that's all.' Ruth gave a shrug and walked over to the door. Then she turned back with a smile and wagged her finger at Esther. 'And make sure you're on your best behaviour. Don't have our new guest surgeon meeting Crabbie Rabbie instead of super midwife Esther.'

Esther looked around for something to throw but Ruth had ducked out the door too early. She shook her head as she walked over to do her checks on her babies and parents.

She'd earned the nickname within a few months of getting here as a student midwife. Because she'd already been qualified as a nurse, she'd caught a few shifts in the wards while completing her midwifery course. Truth was, Esther was never at her best on night shift. That whole 'turn your life upside down for a few days' thing just messed with her body and brain and tended to make her a little cranky—or crabbit as they called it in Scotland.

She'd clashed with one of the junior doctors one night on the ward when he'd continually tried to re-site an IV on an elderly patient, rather than come and ask for help. Once she'd realised he'd had four attempts he hadn't fared well.

The whole ward had heard him getting a dressing-down, her Scottish accent getting thicker by the minute as she got angrier and angrier.

It had been 25 January. Robert Burns Day in Scotland—named after their national poet. This doctor had known that and had walked away muttering, 'Oh, calm down, Crabbie Rabbie,' much to her fury, and the rest of the staff's delight.

She'd never managed to shake it off—even though she mostly kept her temper in check these days.

One of the other staff on shift wandered over. 'Problems?'

She shook her head. 'All stable. I've chased up the x-ray for Billy, just waiting for them to appear. I'm going to take Laura back along to the maternity ward. Her blood sugars are fine and she's starting to grizzle. Must be due a feed.'

'Okay, do that, and then go for first break. You look as if you need it. I'll keep an eye on Billy.'

She laughed and put one hand on her hip. 'I must be looking bad if you're sending me on first break.'

'Go before I change my mind.'

Esther rechecked Billy's obs and chatted with his mum for a few minutes, making sure everything was meticulously recorded and phoning down to Callum again to chase up the x-ray. Then she gathered what she needed for Laura and threw her bag over her shoulder. Ten minutes later, Laura was back at her mother's bedside and happily feeding.

Esther stretched out her back as she headed to the canteen. It didn't normally bother her but today it was aching. Maybe all the extra shifts were taking a toll on her. The smell of freshly baked scones hit her as soon as she walked through the canteen doors. Two minutes later she had a large coffee and an even larger scone with butter and jam before her.

She glanced around the canteen. She couldn't spot Carly or Chloe, the friends that she normally sat with. There was a group of other nurses that she knew, but a seat in the far corner of the room was practically crying out her name. She was too tired to be sociable.

She moved quickly and slid into the seat before anyone else claimed it. Most of the seats were hard-backed and sat around the circular tables in the canteen. But there were a few, slightly more comfortable chairs a little further away—obviously left over from a ward refurb a few years ago.

The scone was gone in minutes and as she sipped her coffee she closed her eyes for just a moment. The door nearest her opened with a bang and a large crowd of people walked in, all talking and laughing at the tops of their voices.

She gritted her teeth. Just five minutes of peace. That's all she wanted. She shifted uncomfortably on the chair, pulling her scrub top from her skin. It seemed unusually warm in here.

The noise continued. Esther watched through

half-shut eyes. There was a guy at the centre of it all. Handsome, in a TV doctor kind of way. Tall, broad-shouldered, with dark rumpled hair. The rest of the people around him seemed to be hanging on his every word, occasionally throwing in a word of their own as if they hoped to garner some approval. Maybe he *was* some kind of TV doc?

'This place is a hospital, not a blooming circus,' she muttered.

She checked the clock on the canteen wall. Five minutes. She had another five minutes left of break time. Esther usually never bothered with timings. Most days she grabbed some food, bolted it down and went straight back to the NICU. But she couldn't believe how tired she felt—it was unusual for her, she did extra shifts frequently and never felt like this—so, for once, she settled back into the chair. For once, she would take her full break.

'Esther, Esther!'

The voice came out of nowhere. Esther jerked awake. Liz, the admin assistant from NICU, was shaking her shoulder. 'Wake up.'

Esther sprang from her seat, knocking the still-full coffee cup that had been balanced on the edge of her chair, splashing coffee up the legs of her scrubs and sending Liz jumping backwards.

'Oh no,' she groaned. She gave herself a shake and glanced at the clock on the wall. She was more than fifteen minutes late.

Liz pulled a face. 'Abi told me to come and find you. The surgeon's arrived. He's reviewing Billy right now.'

Esther stared down at the rapidly spreading stain on the lino beneath her feet. 'Leave it,' Liz said, waving her hand. 'I'll get it. You just go.'

Esther put her hand on Liz's arm. 'Thanks, Liz. I'm so sorry. I'll make it up to you.'

She dashed back down the corridor towards NICU, crashing through the doors and heading straight to the sink to wash her hands. Abi was standing in the middle of a crowd of strangers that must include the new surgeon; she raised her eyebrows and said in a louder than normal voice, 'Oh, good, Billy's midwife is here. She'll be able to update you.'

Esther dried her hands and moved over quickly, making her way through the crowd. 'Hi there, I'm Esther McDonald.' She looked around trying to decide which one of the many bodies wearing white coats must belong to the surgeon. All she knew was he was male. Abi handed over Billy's chart and Esther could see from a glance that he'd had his chest x-ray and his tube feeding had restarted while she'd been gone. She breathed a sigh of relief.

'You're the midwife?'

The deep voice was practically at her ear and she jumped, stumbling over her own feet.

She spun around. Mr Imposing was standing in her personal space, his arms folded across his chest, looking her up and down in a disapproving manner. Okay, so the NICU probably wasn't big enough for all these people, which could explain the space thing. And the massive splatter of coffee all over her scrub trousers probably wasn't helping her appearance.

But right now she could smell his clean aftershave and see into those toffee-coloured eyes.

'Weren't you the nurse who was sleeping in the canteen?'

She could feel the blood rush to her face and all the hairs on her body prickle in indignation. Who did this guy think he was, sweeping in here with his giant entourage?

Nope. No way.

'I'm sure you know that we limit visitors to NICU. Maybe other NICUs relax rules for you and your entourage, but the Queen Victoria doesn't.'

She started to count in her head just how many people were in his little gang. She'd reached twelve when his deep voice sounded right in front of her again.

'Isn't this a teaching hospital? Famous the

world over for its training programmes?' There was a mocking tone in his voice.

Esther had been around long enough to recognise an arrogant doctor. As a nurse, and a midwife, she'd met more than her fair share—both male and female.

She hated anyone being dismissive with her. And she didn't stand for it. More than once she'd used her Scottish accent to the best of her ability to give someone short shrift.

There was something about her accent that generally made people take a step back—particularly when she was angry. If this guy didn't watch out, he'd soon find out exactly who Esther McDonald was. She'd barely had a chance to look this guy up. All she knew was he was one of a few specialist surgeons who could do the procedure that Billy needed.

She mirrored his stance and folded her arms, tilting her chin towards him as she put a fake smile on her face. 'Maybe you'd like to introduce yourself and let me know why you think your needs are more important than the needs of the very special babies we have in here?'

She could do sarcasm too.

He inhaled deeply, almost like he wanted to show her just how broad his chest was. But Esther had never been easily intimidated by anyone. 'I'm Harry Beaumont. I'm here to do the surgery on your patient.'

She raised her eyebrows and nodded. 'Ah, so *you're* here to do the surgery on Billy.' She pointed one finger at him. 'In that case, *you* can stay. Everyone else can wait outside. Unless you've brought your own anaesthetist with you.' She shrugged. 'If you have, then he, or she, can stay too.'

Eleven other faces exchanged anxious glances, so Esther turned her head a few times as she spoke. 'The babies in here are just too susceptible to infection to have this many people around. Visitors are strictly limited, for good reason.' She looked at them all. 'As I don't know who any of you are—and to be honest, I'm a bit funny about letting people I don't know into my NICU too—I'm just going to assume that you're all either medical professionals or trainees, therefore I don't need to explain the principles of infection control to you, so you'll all completely understand that this amount of people is overkill—' she turned her head back towards Harry '—even for a surgeon.'

She'd spoken quite a lot, but knew entirely that all the emphasis was on the things she hadn't said, but had left implied.

There was a tic at the side of Harry's jaw. He was mad. She didn't care. She wanted to tug at her scrub top again. NICUs were always really warm, but this amount of people in close proximity was making her sweat. But tugging at the top would mean she'd have to unfold her arms and that would be a sign of weakness. So not happening.

It was the longest pause. Harry gave the tiniest nod of his head. 'Francesca, will you stay with me, please? The rest of you, if you wait outside we'll find a teaching area where I can explain things in due course.'

Francesca was a petite redhead who was grinning conspiratorially at Esther. She let the rest of the entourage leave, then asked, 'Can I see Billy's films? I'd like to review them before we examine him.'

'Of course,' said Esther, gesturing for both of them to follow her to the nearest computer screen. 'Have you been assigned temporary log-in credentials?'

'I have,' said Harry, moving over next to her and tapping his details in.

It only took a few moments for a scowl to come over his face. 'I sent a list of tests to be completed for Billy before I got here. Some are missing.'

'They are?' Esther moved closer, checking the screen. She'd checked before she'd gone off shift yesterday when there were just a few still to be completed. Ruth had said the rest had been done. What was missing?

She turned to Harry. 'What is it that you're looking for?'

'His bloods. From this morning.'

Of course. 'I'm sure they were done—they've probably not been reported on yet. Don't worry, I can phone the lab and put a rush on them.'

Harry straightened and gave her an incredulous glance. 'What do you mean you're "sure they were done"? You mean you don't actually know? And why wasn't there already a rush put on them?'

She stiffened. He was speaking to her as if she was incompetent. Of course she should know if Billy's bloods had been done or not. But the specialist phlebotomist would have been here while Esther was on her break. If she hadn't been late back, she might have had a chance to check…

She kept her face blank. Her back was aching. 'The orders for the bloods were put in last night. At that point, you hadn't told us when you were coming, or let us know if you'd secured theatre time for Billy. If you had, there would have been a rush put on his bloods.'

She moved over to the desk to pick up the phone. Every word he'd said had annoyed her. But what irked most was that they felt true.

What was wrong with her? She prided herself

on being meticulous at work. It wasn't like she'd made any kind of mistake but…in her brain it *almost* felt like that. Double-checking things was second nature to her.

'I'm used to working with professionals. I guess the standards here are not what I'm used to.'

'Excuse me?' She couldn't help herself. There was no way she going to let anyone accuse her of being unprofessional. It was the biggest slight that someone could say to a nurse or midwife.

But it seemed that Harry was off on a rant. He kept his voice low, so that no one else in the unit could hear. 'Why does Billy still have a feeding tube in situ? In order for Francesca to anaesthetise him, she needs to ensure his stomach is empty. His feeding should have stopped a few hours ago.'

Now Esther wanted to shout at him, but just at that moment a voice answered at the end of the phone. 'Lab,' came the weary response.

Something inside Esther panged. Whoever was working there was obviously every bit as tired as she was. 'It's Esther from NICU. Can I chase bloods for a baby that's going to Theatre?'

There was a sigh and murmur of consent. She replaced the receiver and turned to face Francesca, completely ignoring Mr Entourage. She wasn't even prepared to use his name right now.

'If you refresh the screen in around five minutes Billy's bloods will be available. One of the machines was down for a few hours this morning but it's back up and running now. Billy's bloods had already been in the system. They're just waiting for his clotting factor.'

Francesca gave a nod. 'Perfect.'

Esther looked at Harry's screen. He was looking at the cardiac echo that had been taken yesterday. Billy needed his surgery, badly.

She moved alongside Harry. 'I have many skills, Mr Beaumont, but mind reading isn't one of them. Like I said earlier, if you'd given us notice of Billy's procedure, then we'd have made sure his feeds were stopped in good time. As it was, his tube dislodged last night and had to be replaced. Billy already had a few hours without sustenance, while his tube was re-sited and then checked. His feed only started again in the last hour.' She braced herself and turned her head towards him. 'And for me, unprofessional is a surgeon sweeping into a NICU with an entourage of twelve people with no regard for the patients or parents who are already in a stressful environment. For a surgeon with your apparent experience, I'd expect better.'

Harry was trying his absolute best to keep his temper in check, but this midwife was trying his patience in every possible way. It didn't help that she had a cheek to be angry at him, or that when she was clearly annoyed she spoke so quickly he had to concentrate to make out a single word that she said. Her Scottish accent was fierce. A bit like she was.

By rights she should probably have fiery red hair to match. But she didn't. She had dark hair that was up in a ponytail, and her skin looked as though it had once been tanned but was now strangely pale. He couldn't possibly ignore the dark circles under her blue eyes, or the dirty scrubs she was wearing. He wasn't quite sure what all this meant—apart from the fact she was looking after the baby he was due to take to Theatre.

Harry had spent his life in and out of NICUs across the world due to his surgical speciality. There weren't many people that wanted to work on such tiny hearts and veins—particularly when the tissues were so fragile and these little lives could literally be on a knife edge.

What the staff in the NICU at the Queen Victoria clearly didn't know was that he was the new visiting surgeon, which meant that, where possible, babies with heart conditions would be brought here for him to operate on. For those who were too sick to travel any distance, he would still go to them. But having a semipermanent base with a team around him would be good. He'd hoped to find professional colleagues he could trust and rely on. But first impressions of this midwife weren't exactly good.

There was no way he wanted her watching Billy postsurgery.

But what annoyed him most of all was the way she'd quickly and determinedly told him to get his staff out of 'her' NICU.

And she'd been right. They always tried to reduce the amount of close contacts that prem babies had. It was important. Their immune systems were often not fully developed, and most humans were walking petri dishes.

People could be carrying bugs for days without any signs or symptoms. Something that caused a mere sniffle in an adult could be deadly to a premature baby. It might be a teaching hospital but even he wouldn't expect any NICU to let in that many students and trainees. He'd been in such a hurry to get in here and see his patient, and been so swept away by the enthusiasm of the staff at his side, that he hadn't stopped to think. And Harry didn't make mistakes like that. So being called on it was embarrassing.

'You must have known Billy was going to Theatre today,' he said briskly to the midwife.

She gave him a weary look that told him she was getting very bored by all this. 'I *hoped* you might show your face today. I hoped that Billy wouldn't have to wait another day for surgery. I was told that you were *supposed* to turn up today, but no one knew when. I look after both baby and mum, and if you'd communicated a little better, there was also the chance I could have prepared mum more for his surgery today.'

She put her hands at the back of both hips, leaned backwards and winced as if she'd touched something painful.

'Blood results are in,' said Francesca in a manner that could only be described as deliberately distracting. It was clear she was trying to break the tension between them. 'His blood gases are a little lower than I would have liked. But not anything I wouldn't have expected.' Francesca gave a little sigh and Harry felt a rush of sympathy for her. They'd worked together for a long time. She was a great anaesthetist. It took great skill to manage these tiny babies in Theatre and he depended on her completely. Francesca's chair scraped on the ground as she stood up. 'I need to sound his chest. Let me wash up first.'

He followed her over to the sink in the treatment room, completely sidestepping Esther and washing his hands too. He needed to prioritise this baby, not the midwife who looked as if she could currently fall asleep on her feet.

As he stepped back his arm brushed against

hers and she jerked away. But not before he noticed how hot she was. 'Do you have some kind of infection?'

She looked shocked. 'What?'

'You're burning up. What's your temperature?' His arm swept out across all the cribs in the NICU. 'If you have anything respiratory you're putting the lives of all these babies at risk.'

'I don't have anything respiratory,' she snapped. 'My chest is clear as a bell.'

For one strange second he realised that her words had made him look exactly at her breasts hidden under her scrubs. He turned back to Francesca. 'We should see this baby on our own.'

Esther stepped into his path. 'No, you won't. I know Jill, his mum, best. She needs support. She trusts me.'

Harry glared at her and she held up her hands. 'Okay, I won't touch Billy, right now. I'll run down to A&E when you're done and get a clean bill of health. But you don't see him without me.'

Harry pressed his lips together, stopping himself from just getting into a pointless argument. 'Only speak to mum, then,' he reiterated.

She gave an exasperated nod and held out her hand. 'This way.'

Harry and Francesca followed her over to the left-hand side of the unit to where a young woman sat staring at her baby lying in the crib and rocking backwards and forward in the nursing chair. Harry had dealt with lots of anxious parents. NICUs were the most intimidating places on earth. Parents frequently felt everything was out of their control, and he was used to comforting and supporting parents who were overwhelmed with helplessness and focused on every word that was said to them. This mother was young. Her lank hair was pulled back from her face. It looked as if it hadn't been washed for a while and from first appearance he actually wondered when she'd last eaten. Now he understood just why Esther was being so protective of Billy's mum. It was clear she didn't have many support systems in place.

'Jill, this is Harry Beaumont. He's the surgeon that's going to do the surgery on Billy.'

Harry crouched down so he was level with Jill. She'd sat forward but hadn't stood up. He gave her a broad smile. 'It's a pleasure to meet you, Jill. I'm here to take a look at Billy. I'm hoping we'll be able to take him for surgery later today. Do you mind if I examine him?'

Jill paused for a few moments as her eyes filled with tears, then she gave a tiny nod. 'Of course.'

She was terrified. He got that. Harry used some of the NICU hand sanitiser before opening the crib to examine Billy, while Francesca introduced herself as Billy's anaesthetist. He could tell straight away that Esther completely understood, and after a few moments, he could see the tension in Jill's shoulders start to dissolve as he spoke to Billy in a calm, quiet voice as he examined him.

'Hi, Billy, I'm here to see how you're doing. Let's have a little listen to your heart and lungs.' He took his time, listening carefully, then checking his oxygen sats, his feeding tube and his colour. Babies this small frequently had skin that was almost translucent. Their circulatory systems—and particularly Billy's—weren't functioning quite right, and they often couldn't regulate their temperatures. Operating and anaesthetising these babies carried huge risks. He gave Francesca a nod as he moved his stethoscope back to Billy's chest. 'Want to take a listen?'

She nodded and moved alongside him. There was no point her touching Billy too when she really just needed to listen to his heart and lungs. So, she listened through Harry's stethoscope, nudging him to move it on occasion.

Harry could sense Esther watching them curiously. She wouldn't know they'd done this a dozen times before. As Francesca finished her examination it struck him how similar Esther and Jill looked. Exhausted and tired. He could understand it for the mother. But for a member of staff—it wasn't good enough.

Francesca gave him a nod and he removed his stethoscope and pulled a chair over next to Jill and spent the next few minutes explaining Billy's surgery to her in simple terms. He brought out some notes that he'd prepared earlier. He always gave the parents of the babies he operated on some clear notes that they could refer to later. Experience had taught him that although parents listened, anxiety meant that they didn't always remember or understand what they'd been told.

He could feel Esther's eyes on him the whole time. He would expect the midwife assigned to this child to listen to his explanation. It would mean that she could reiterate anything to the mum at a later date. But somehow, today, it irked him. And he couldn't quite understand why.

'Do you have any questions?' he checked with Jill. She shook her head and he gave her a small nod. 'If you think of anything later I'll still be available to answer any questions. I'm going to organise some theatre time now. I hope to take Billy later this afternoon. We'll stop his feeding for the next few hours, and I'd expect the surgery to last around six hours. You can come down to Theatre if you want while Billy goes to sleep, and I'll come and find you as soon as we're finished to update on how things have gone. Okay?'

Jill gave a nod.

'I'm just going to have a chat with your midwife, and then I'll talk to you in a while and get you to sign the consent forms.'

He smiled and walked back over to the nurses' station with Francesca and Esther. Francesca sat down and started making some notes. Esther turned to look at him. 'You aren't doing the consent form now?'

He shook his head. 'No. I've given her a lot to process. I want to give her a bit of time to think about everything I've told her before I get her to sign the consent form. She might have more questions later.'

Esther gave a brief nod.

He narrowed his gaze. Was she actually listening? He glanced at the board he'd noticed yesterday. It was a shift rota for staff.

The next few days would be vital for Billy. It was important that whoever was looking after him was at the top of their game. Esther's name was on the rota for tomorrow. He couldn't let that go.

'You're tired. No, scrap that, you're exhausted. And I think you're sick. I don't think you should be at work and I certainly don't think you should be assigned to Billy. For the next few days he's going to need someone who's alert and on their game.' He paused for the briefest second, because he knew what he was about to say wasn't exactly nice. 'And to be honest, I'm not convinced that's you. I want another midwife assigned to Billy.'

'What?' Well, that had certainly gotten her attention.

'I'm sorry. But I can't take the risk of performing this surgery and having his postoperative care compromised.'

'How dare you!' she hissed at him. She glanced down. 'What? Because I have a little coffee spilled on my scrubs and I haven't had a chance to get changed yet, and because I dared to close my eyes in the hospital canteen, you've decided I'm not fit to do my job? Just who do you think you are?'

He cringed. He hadn't exactly said those words but it was certainly how he'd felt. 'I think you're sick,' he said quickly. 'I think you might need to be checked over, and have a few days' rest.' He could see a couple of other staff members looking their way—as if they'd picked up that something was wrong. The last thing he wanted when he was taking up a position here was to cause a ruckus with the staff.

'My priority is my patient,' he said quietly but firmly.

'And mine isn't?' He could tell she was mad.

That wasn't what he meant, even though he'd clearly just implied it. But then again, did he really want this midwife looking after his patient if she wasn't at the top of her game?

Francesca glared at him from over her computer. Oh no. That didn't usually happen. Francesca normally had his back.

He took a deep breath. 'Esther, I have to call things the way I see it. I think you're running a temp and maybe need to take some time off. You agreed you'd go down to A&E and get checked over. Why don't you do that and we'll take it from there.' It was a compromise. But it was the best he could do right now.

She kept her face entirely straight and pulled up a few things on the computer and grabbed the chart from the base of Billy's crib.

'Here, Mr Beaumont. I'd like you to check my work. Here's all the orders I made for Billy on my shifts for the last few days. Here's all my nursing notes. Here's every temp, blood pressure, pulse and respiratory rate. Here's his medications I've administered, and his feeding. Here's his skin care chart. Here's his colour chart. Here's how many times I've sounded his chest to ensure that it remains clear. Here is exactly how many times he's had a wet or dirty nappy.' She pulled up a final chart. 'And here's how many times I've had to chase doctors, other departments, test results…all to ensure Billy's care is up to my standards.' She held herself very still, but there was the tiniest tremble in her voice. 'I want you to take the time to look at what I've done. Because I record everything, *meticulously*.' She emphasized the word, then gave a wave of her hand. 'And once you've done that, I can pull up all the same information for his mother, and you can check my recordings for Jill too.' She paused for a few seconds as he glanced over what she'd handed him. 'Unfortunately I'm not on shift twenty-four hours a day, so I've only given you what I've done for Billy. Hospitals have emergencies, as I'm sure you're aware. Blood machines break down. Feeding tubes dislodge and can't be safely used again until there's been an x-ray that's been checked by a physician. I'm not responsible for other people's time constraints.'

He was checking. She was right. He couldn't deny it. Her recording was meticulous. Some of the best he'd ever seen, and he'd been in a *lot* of NICU units.

She'd felt warm to the touch earlier, but as she'd moved closer as she spoke to him he couldn't hear any sign of a wheeze or rasp in her breathing. Every person was different. Maybe she didn't have an infection. Maybe he was overreacting. It could be that her body temperature just ran at the top end of normal. It happened.

What was clear was he couldn't tell her why he'd overreacted. He couldn't tell her that deep down there was an underlying paranoia about his patients and their welfare.

Before he could blink she'd stepped right up in front of him, her accent thick but perfectly legible. 'You know, Harry, I'm actually glad that you're here. Because even though you're an insufferably arrogant fool, I know how much Billy needs this surgery. And I put him first. Always. But I'm only going to say this once. Don't *ever* talk to me like that again and don't *ever* question my professionalism or my competency at work.' She put both hands on her hips. 'I wish you luck with Billy's surgery today, but after that, I hope I never have to see your sorry ass in here again.' And with that, she turned on her heel and walked away, leaving Harry feeling about as welcome as a thorn in a space suit.

Francesca tutted and gave him a sarcastic smile. 'Well done, Harry. First day on a new job and you've made friends.' She picked up her bag. 'And to be honest,' she said in a low voice as she walked past. 'Against her? I don't fancy your chances at all.'

CHAPTER TWO

THE SIGNS HAD been there but she'd been too busy to pick them up—looking after Jill, worrying about her mum. Esther cursed herself all the way down the stairs towards A&E. She hated the fact that it took that pompous prince, duke or whatever he claimed to be to point them out before the penny had finally dropped for her.

Abi had told her to go on down for the check while she took care of Billy but Esther already knew exactly what was wrong with her. She'd ducked into the treatment room and took her own temperature. Yip. She was burning up. She grabbed some paracetamol from her handbag. She had to start somewhere.

Rob, one of the advanced nurse practitioners, was at the nurses' station in the middle of the A&E department. He took one look. 'You okay?'

She shook her head. 'I think I've got an upper UTI. Can I borrow you for five minutes?'

He nodded. 'Sure.' Then he smiled and handed her a specimen bottle. 'Let's get you sorted.'

It took a little more than five minutes because Rob liked to be thorough. Once he heard her past history of having kidney problems as a child, leaving her prone to upper urinary tract infections, he gave a little nod, dipsticked her urine, rechecked her temp and listened to her symptoms of fatigue and an aching lower back.

'You couldn't come down earlier?'

She sighed. 'I'd felt a bit tired but my back only started aching this morning and the new neonatal cardiac surgeon arrived today so I've been flat out dealing with him too.'

He gave her a nod and scribbled some notes. 'What normally works best?'

She told him the name of the antibiotic that normally resolved her infections and he scribbled a prescription, then went to one of the cupboards and pulled out a bottle, signing a form to record it. 'Okay, so I won't make you trek to the pharmacy. But I'm still sending your sample away to make sure you're on the right antibiotic. Results should be on the system tomorrow. I'm working then—will I give you a call?'

Esther gave a grateful nod. The computer system in the Queen Victoria meant that no staff could access their own records or results—no matter how tempting it was. 'Perfect. Thanks, Rob.'

'Any time. Not many perks to being in the NHS. We've got to look after our own. Are you going to take some time off?'

'Me?' She smiled and shook her head. 'As soon as I start taking these, they usually work fast. This time tomorrow I'll start to feel better. I'll just take some paracetamol until then.'

He gave a nod. 'Fine, but let me know if there's anything else you need.'

'An assassination attempt on a visiting surgeon, maybe?'

Rob looked up in surprise. 'He's annoyed Crabbie Rabbie? Wow, he's brave.'

She waved her hand. 'Don't worry. I've told him how much I love him already. Hopefully he'll do his surgery, fix my baby and leave.'

She gave Rob a nod and disappeared out the cubicle and back along the corridor. In a way she was happy. This had obviously been working on her for the last few days. At least now she knew why she was so unnaturally tired. It was sort of a relief to know that after a few days of antibiotics she'd be back to herself again.

As she pushed open the door, the manager of the A&E department was heading towards her.

Shirley had her hands full, so Esther held the door for her.

She gave her a grin. 'Lifesaver, thanks.'

'No probs.'

Something flitted across Shirley's face. 'Hey, don't suppose you could cover a shift on Thursday?'

Esther glanced at the pill bottle she'd just pushed into the pocket of her uniform. Thursday. Three days away. It was her next scheduled day off and she was bound to be feeling better by then. 'Sure.' She nodded.

'Great,' Shirley shouted over her shoulder as she continued to speed down the corridor.

Harry was doing his absolute best not to try and cause trouble. Only because Francesca had torn a few strips off him.

'You were way out of line yesterday,' she said quietly as they met the next morning.

'How was I out of line? I don't want some flaky member of staff caring for my baby.'

'Your baby?' Francesca raised her eyebrows.

He sighed. 'You know what I mean. If I operate on them, they're all my babies.'

'Don't try the mushy stuff with me. You're being harsh. So, she spilt coffee and didn't have time to change. Who hasn't? Half the times I was called to a cardiac arrest, I went with half my lunch down me.'

'Did you sleep in the hospital canteen too?'

Francesca shrugged. 'Sometimes. If I'd been up all night on call, I might grab five minutes when I had to. Can you really say that you've never done that?'

He took in a deep breath and gave a conciliatory shrug too. 'Okay, I might have.'

Francesca gave him a hard stare. 'I'm just saying. This is the first time you've operated here. I'd try not to get on the wrong side of everyone you might come across if you're going to be a visiting surgeon.'

'Now who's being harsh?'

Francesca started pulling up some results on a nearby computer. 'Anyway. I would tread carefully. I've heard she's got a nickname.'

'A nickname?'

Francesca nodded and smiled. 'Yep. Crabbie Rabbie.'

'What?' Harry frowned.

'Something to do with Scotland's national bard?'

'I know who Rabbie Burns is.'

'Well, apparently she got the nickname just after she arrived. Something to do with her strong accent and the fact she takes no prisoners with people she thinks are annoying.'

'Are you trying to tell me something?'

'Just that I think you've clearly just put your-self into the annoying category.'

He shook his head. 'Oh, thanks for that.' The door to the NICU opened and the day staff filed in, Esther among them.

Her dark hair was swept up in an elaborate plait. She still looked tired but maybe she'd put a little more make-up on, because there was more colour in her cheeks than there had been yes-terday. She was wearing a different colour of scrubs today. Bright pink. He'd noticed the staff in the NICU wore different colours—sometimes even with child-friendly designs. The brighter colour made her not look quite so washed out.

It was odd. On any other day—with any other member of staff—he might actually have admit-ted that he thought she was quite attractive. But he didn't have time for that. Harry didn't usu-ally date anyone from work. Too many compli-cations. And he and Esther hadn't exactly got off to a good start.

He wanted to ask if she was fit to work. He wanted to ask if she still had a temperature. He knew he wasn't entitled to. Staff in NICUs were extremely familiar with the dangers of expos-ing babies to potential infections. He shouldn't second-guess anyone.

Francesca tapped his arm. 'Okay, I'm off to

see another baby.' She shot him another look. 'Now, behave. Play nicely.'

He shook his head as she walked out the door.

Esther had raged last night as she'd tried to get to sleep. It was ridiculous. All day all she'd wanted to do was sleep, but actually put her in comfy pyjamas and give her her own bed and she lay there blinking and plotting horrible futures for that annoying surgeon. The man had even stolen her sleep from her.

She ignored the fact it was noisy outside, the pipes creaked, the radiators hissed and upstairs seemed to be having a party again. Her back might have ached a little too, and she'd needed to pee on numerous occasions. It was funny how when you finally got a diagnosis your body practically slapped you on the face with it. But no, it was none of those things that prevented her from sleeping; it was definitely smug Harry Beaumont with his entourage and unflattering words.

She burned from a few of the things he'd said to her. But most of all was his threat to ask for another midwife to be assigned to Billy. She was pretty sure that the charge nurse for the unit would give him short shrift. Oona was from Northern Ireland, and was much more like Esther in temperament than she cared to admit.

She wouldn't take kindly to some visiting surgeon dictating what happened in her NICU.

But as Esther walked through the door of NICU she could see Harry sitting at the nurses' station. It was 6:50 in the morning and clearly her worst day in the world was just about to start.

It didn't help that he was looking like Dr Delicious in his pale blue shirt that was a little damp around the collar. He'd obviously just showered and was currently charming the few staff around him; they were laughing and joking.

She braced herself, waiting for someone to tell her she couldn't look after the little boy she'd spent the last few days tending to. Her eyes hesitantly went to the board. Esther McDonald was written next to Billy Rudd and Akshita Patel. She let out a sigh of relief and went straight over to hear the report.

Somehow she just knew that every single step of the way Harry's eyes were watching. What was he waiting for?

She pointedly ignored him. Billy's surgery had apparently gone well, which was a relief. She hurried over to his crib to get a look at him for herself, making sure she gave Jill a hug first.

His colour was different—straight away. Some people might not have found it obvious, but Esther was an experienced NICU member of staff and had always noticed the slight dusky tinge to Billy's skin. Today, it was gone. His skin still had the translucence of a premature baby, but the colour had definitely improved.

She breathed and caught a scent. She tensed. She recognised it from yesterday, some kind of woody undertones. Harry. She was determined not to turn around.

Jill had got up and gone into the small kitchen in NICU to make herself a cup of tea.

'Things went well?' she asked Harry in an even tone. They might have got off to a bad start but there was no point in being uncivil.

'Yes, and no,' he said in a low voice.

'What do you mean?'

'I mean, things took a little longer than expected. We ran into some problems. The surgery ended up taking about eight hours.'

Esther turned to face him in shock. She knew how long the surgery should have taken. 'But…'

He shook his head. 'It's all under control. The surgery was successful. Billy will need regular reviews and be carefully monitored for the next few days, but—' he paused and gave a slow nod of his head before his dark eyes met hers '—the next few days will be the most crucial.'

Her skin prickled. He wasn't saying anything out loud. But it felt like he was accusing her of something.

'Experience with these babies tells me that if something is going to go wrong, it generally happens in the first forty-eight hours after surgery.'

The time when she was part of the team watching Billy.

She tilted her chin, part of her felt defiant, and part of her felt distinctly annoyed by his unsaid implication.

She glanced at the clock on the wall. She knew when surgery had started yesterday. If it had taken eight hours, it couldn't have finished until well after midnight. Harry had already been here when she'd come in for her shift. She knew she hadn't slept last night, but had he?

'Are you staying close by? You've had a quick turnaround.'

She wasn't even sure where the observation came from, and the instant it came out her mouth she wasn't entirely comfortable with how it sounded.

But Harry didn't seem to notice. 'I'm only a few miles away in Belgravia, but I stayed here last night to keep an eye on Billy.'

'Oh.' She nodded. Belgravia. Of course. He was supposed to be some kind of royalty, wasn't he? Of course that's where he'd stay. Not like herself, who had to travel nearly an hour each day to get to work.

He pulled something from his pocket, then cleared his throat. 'I left a note for the NICU nurse last night about all the things I wanted monitored in Billy.'

She glanced at the piece of paper in his hand. 'I do know how to do postoperative care, Harry. This isn't my first rodeo, you know.' There was no way she was touching that list. Her eyes quickly ran down it. It was what they would do for every baby postsurgery, with the exception of one test that could easily be ordered with the rest of the blood work.

She pressed her lips together and tried not to snap. Everything about this guy just seemed to annoy her. Even the way his aftershave seemed to linger in the air between them. 'I guess when you move around a lot you don't know what's normal in each NICU. But you don't need to worry about the Queen Victoria. We have a reputation of excellence because we've earned it.'

Was that too pointed? She didn't think so. It seemed more factual to her.

He wasn't wearing a typical doctor white coat and her eyes were drawn to the muscles beneath the pale blue shirt he wore. The shirt was clearly tailored, defining all the parts of him it should. It had short sleeves—just like all doctors were supposed to wear in clinical areas, but the short sleeves drew her attention to his biceps. Some place she definitely didn't need to look.

'Point taken,' said Harry frostily. 'But I'd still like my post-op instructions followed. I don't think that's unreasonable.'

He was still holding the piece of paper towards her. It was like a standoff. She didn't want to take it. She didn't. But Jill came out of the kitchen and started walking towards them. The last thing she needed was for Billy's mum to think there was any kind of issue between the staff looking after her child. Esther reached out and grabbed the paper, stuffing it in her pocket.

'Fine.'

One of his eyebrows quirked upwards. 'Fine,' he agreed before turning and walking away.

She moved quickly, doing her routine checks on Billy, followed by routine checks on the little girl she was taking care of too.

She'd hoped that Harry would take the cue to leave the NICU. Surely he must be tired? Or at the very least have other work to do. But apparently not. He settled in and made himself comfortable in a corner of the NICU, opening up a laptop and sitting next to one of the phones.

The phone calls were brisk. He seemed to consult on a whole host of cases, some in the UK, and some in Europe.

Not that she was listening to what he was

doing. Of course not. She just kept hoping that one of those calls would give him an incentive to actually leave the NICU.

Every time she turned around she felt as if she could feel his eyes on her. At first she told herself it was her imagination. But on the few occasions she looked up, they definitely locked gazes, making heat rush into her cheeks.

She chewed the inside of her cheek as she logged in to one of the patient monitoring systems to update her nursing notes on Billy.

There was a little pink flash in the bottom right-hand corner. Someone else was in these notes. That wasn't too unusual. The lab could be uploading results. Or someone else could be viewing x-rays or ultrasounds. But then the little flash turned blue, and Esther's temperature turned red.

Now, someone was looking at the nursing notes. *Her nursing notes.* The ones she hadn't even written yet. And all of sudden she didn't have a single doubt who it was.

This guy was checking up on her, and that made her mad. She couldn't even remember being supervised this much as a student nurse. When she'd come to the Queen Victoria to do her additional midwifery training it had only taken a few shifts for the staff she worked with to realise she was already trained as a nurse and was clearly competent. Of course, labour and deliveries were supervised. But when she was giving out regular medicines and writing up notes, the staff didn't need to double-check as she already had a professional registration. So this definitely felt like being under the microscope. And she didn't like it—not one bit.

The temptation to write *Get Lost* in the electronic system was overwhelming. It would appear to him in live time. Unfortunately this system was designed to keep a permanent log of everything recorded. So, if she typed it once— even if she deleted it a few seconds later—it could always be pulled up on a previous search.

It was designed to stop users changing records at a later date, but had actually proved a fail-safe for one midwife who'd accidentally recorded notes in the wrong patient record, deleted them, then had to deal with an emergency. The timing had meant she'd totally forgotten to go back and add the notes into the correct patient record. When questions had been asked later, the system could prove the record had been made, just not in the right place.

The midwife still got into trouble, just not as much as she could have.

Esther ignored Harry. She had to. Instead, she quickly typed Billy's latest observations and results, along with a few thoughts of her own.

Then she flipped into the records for Jill and made a few notes too. Jill was also still under observation and Esther had a few concerns.

An hour later, Harry was back by her side. He didn't speak, but his shoes came into her line of vision. Italian handmade leather shoes. Something she'd only ever seen on movie stars before. Even his shoes annoyed her.

Was she maybe being irrational?

She waited until he'd sounded Billy's chest again. 'Why were you checking my notes?'

His hands flinched. 'I wasn't specifically checking your notes, Esther.'

'You were. I can tell when someone is looking at the page I'm on.'

He gave her a sideways glance. 'I was reviewing all of Billy's records. From his delivery, to his first films, his consecutive test results and *all* of his medical and nursing notes. I like to be cautious. I like to take a big-picture look at my patients.' He turned to face her. He gave her a reluctant kind of look. 'I often think that the observations of the midwives or nurses that care for the patients are the most important. They might notice things that other people miss.' He paused and ran one hand through his thick rumpled hair. There was something about that motion. The look on his face as he did it that made her breath catch somewhere at the back of her throat. Sorrow. Pain. Regret.

'I've found over the years when we've had to do significant adverse event reviews, or even child death reviews, that often in case notes we can pick up tiny comments that might not seem like much to begin with, but when you stop—' he held up his hands and swept them around '—and look at the whole picture, they all prove to be part of the jigsaw puzzle. The one that we often don't put together until it's far too late.' He bit his bottom lip… There was something about this; she could tell he was keeping his emotions in check, and it made her stop feeling quite so angry at him. He took a deep breath. 'So, I've learned to pay attention. To read all the notes—by everybody involved—and keep everything in mind.' His toffee eyes locked on hers. 'Because what's the point in doing all these reviews if we don't actually learn anything from them?'

Her mouth had gone dry. There was so much more to this story. Yes, she felt under the spotlight by him. Yes, she felt as if his words yesterday had been unjustified. But now he was telling her exactly why he was being meticulous, and her previously irritated brain could absolutely understand it.

He worked around a variety of hospitals. It was doubtful that he could remember anyone's name. Everyone knew that some hospital units were better run than others. Esther could write a list right now of places she would never apply for a permanent position. Was it any wonder he didn't think twice about handing over written instructions postsurgery for a patient?

Maybe she was letting her annoyance with him yesterday colour her judgement.

He was still standing there. Just a few steps away from her. She could see the rise and fall of his chest under his tailored shirt. The shirt that probably cost more than any outfit in her closet at home.

It was hard not to see the differences between them both. His cut-glass accent both annoyed and intrigued her. What was it really like to be a member of the upper classes? She was pretty sure she'd never met anyone before who would fall into that category. Had Harry been guaranteed a place at one of the best medical schools as part of his birthright? Or was all that outdated nonsense? She really had no clue.

What she was sure about was that he hadn't had to juggle school work with two part-time jobs at school, and study into the late hours to make the grades he needed. Esther wasn't some natural genius. She'd worked hard to get what she needed to get into university in Scotland. Doing the conversion course to midwifery in

London had only been possible because of a grant from a Scottish millionaire who stayed in her area and invited Scots people to apply. Scotland was one of the few places on the planet where university tuition was free for their kids. But if a Scots kid wanted to do a course that was only offered in England? Then, like everyone else, they had to pay. She'd only been able to get to the Queen Victoria through getting the grant to fund her fees. It had also covered her rent during her training, so she was much luckier than most. But somehow she knew that Harry Beaumont had never had to worry about tuition fees or accommodation in his life.

Her mind drifted. Wondering if he'd ever been to Buckingham Palace or knew anyone there. Maybe he'd been best friends with one of the younger princes? He'd be around the same age.

Esther's eyes fixated on his arms again. The muscles made her wonder if he was a rower. That would be it. He'd probably been part of either Oxford or Cambridge's row teams.

There was a soft cough to her left and she jerked, turning to see Jill watching her with a strange expression on her face.

'Everything okay?'

Jill looked between them both. 'That's just what I was about to ask you. You both seem to have been here awhile. Is there something wrong with Billy?'

Harry automatically stepped backwards. 'No, no, everything is fine. I'm very pleased with Billy's progress.'

He seemed to rethink his words. 'Of course, we're still going to keep monitoring him closely for the next few days. But, so far, he's making a good recovery.'

Esther felt a tiny flash of something. The way he'd retreated from his initial words. It was almost like he didn't want to seem too confident that Billy was out of the woods. Not to give Jill too many reassurances that could lead her to think that nothing else could go wrong.

She wondered if Jill had even noticed. But it didn't really matter because Esther had. She put her hands on her hips and gave a little stretch backwards. It was odd. She was still having to take paracetamol for her temperature and she had still had that odd heavy feeling. Usually by this point the antibiotics would have started to kick in, and the tiredness at least would have begun to lift.

But not yet.

Her appetite hadn't quite returned either. Yesterday she'd ate that scone, and then hadn't eaten until later at night—and that had just been a bowl of soup. This morning she hadn't even eaten breakfast, just made do with a caramel latte. That had been on the way into work, and funny thing was, she still wasn't hungry.

She gave Jill a smile. 'How you doing? I'll be going to the canteen later for some food. Want to come with me?'

It didn't matter whether she was hungry or not. Some of the other staff had noted that Jill hadn't been eating much. Hospital meals were always supplied for parents in the NICU, but Jill hadn't been touching hers. She did occasionally leave the NICU and say she was going to buy something—usually from a vending machine— but Esther wasn't convinced. Maybe it was time to try another tack.

Jill shot a glance at the crib. 'But if you're with me, who will watch Billy?' There was genuine apprehension in her voice.

'I will,' came the deep reply without hesitation. 'I intend to be around most of the day, so let me know when you both want to go, and I'll make myself a coffee, and take up post in the most comfortable chair in the place.'

He pointed to the reclining chair that Jill had next to Billy's crib and she let out a laugh. Not all of the chairs in the unit could tip back the way Jill's did and she was the envy of some of the other parents. 'You promise you won't leave him?' She looked over at Esther, then turned back to Harry. 'I know all the staff are good, but I trust Esther the most. I only ever leave Billy for more than a few minutes if she's here.'

He held up his hands, laughing. 'So what am I? The sloppy second?'

Colour rushed into Jill's cheeks but Esther quickly took a step towards Harry and nudged him. 'That's what I like. A surgeon that knows his place.' She couldn't hide the glint in her eye.

They'd definitely started off on the wrong foot together, but she was beginning to understand him just a little more. He might not be quite as arrogant as she'd first thought. As if right on cue her stomach gave a grumble.

'Oh,' said Jill. 'Shall we go now? Let me grab my bag.'

Esther put her hands to her stomach and let out an embarrassed laugh. 'Oops.'

'Better make my coffee, then,' said Harry quickly as he ducked into the NICU kitchen.

Esther went to check with one of her other colleagues that it was fine to leave. 'Harry's apparently watching Billy,' she told her.

Danielle raised her eyebrows. 'The surgeon? How on earth did you manage that one?'

'I didn't,' she said, feeling a little uncomfortable. It was unusual. She couldn't remember a surgeon ever offering to keep watch on a baby. Not to cover a break at least. 'He offered.' She paused for a second, then added, 'I think he's concerned about mum. I offered to take Jill down to the canteen but she was reluctant to go and leave Billy.'

'Ah. That makes sense. Try and get her a bit of fresh air too. She needs it.' It was almost like Danielle had instantly forgotten the first part of the conversation. She stuck her hand in her pocket and pulled out some coins. 'Here, get me something sweet. This diet I've been on is killing me. I need a chocolate fix.'

Esther smiled and nodded. 'No probs. See you soon.'

She checked back at the crib. Harry had settled into the seat and had pulled the flap down on the crib and was talking in a quiet voice to Billy. As she walked over he pretended not to notice. 'Watch out, Billy. Here comes Crabbie Rabbie. We've got to behave around her or we'll both get into trouble.'

Esther's mouth hung open. 'Who on earth told you that?' She'd always known her nickname. Her colleagues frequently used it with affection, but she hadn't expected some visiting surgeon to come out with it. People had clearly been talking.

'What?' Now it was his turn to have the glint in his eyes. He glanced over each shoulder as if someone was standing behind him. 'Did I say something?'

She leaned at the edge of the crib and looked down at Billy. 'Billy, don't you listen to these bad influences. You know who the favourite is.'

She touched Harry's shoulder on the way past. 'And you're right. You do have to behave. Don't forget it.'

Jill hurried over with her bag on her shoulder. 'Are we good to go?'

Harry smiled. 'Absolutely, your boy is in safe hands. Now take your time. I'll be right here waiting.'

He shot Esther a quick glance. A silent message passing between them. Their joking was pushed aside again. Jill was the priority here. There was so much evidence about healthy mum, healthy baby. Esther took it completely seriously, and it seemed like Harry did too.

Esther held open the door for Jill, taking one final glance backwards as something warm spread through her. Most surgeons she met were quite insular. Only interested in moving on to their next surgery once the job was done. Harry seemed to be taking a much wider view. It was nice.

His head was dipped close to Billy and he was chatting away, his cup on the table next to him. She watched as he used some gel nearby before stretching his hand inside and letting Billy grasp his finger.

A smile lit up Harry's face.

And that was the moment she knew he was trouble.

CHAPTER THREE

SHE DIDN'T SLEEP too well that night. She might as well have covered the night shift the amount of times she was back and forth to the toilet.

By the time she took the route along the Thames she'd reached that strange point where sleep now seemed like an optional extra, so she bought the biggest coffee she could from one of the street vendors with two extra shots to try and give herself the oomph that felt missing.

It was a huge relief when she walked into the NICU and Harry wasn't there. Last thing she wanted was him calling her on how tired she looked. Apparently he'd gone back to France to see the baby he'd operated on previously.

He'd been so scrupulous about Billy's monitoring—almost as much as she was—and she'd heard him on the phone to France yesterday on a few occasions. It was clear he kept a close eye on any baby he'd operated on.

Yesterday they seemed to have reached an

uneasy truce. There hadn't been a single word about her expertise or competence. She'd spent most of the day looking after both Billy and his mother, but Harry had constantly stayed around. Lingering doubts had hovered in her head and part of her wondered if he was keeping an eye on Billy, or if he was really keeping an eye on her. The more she'd thought about it last night, the more it seemed to amplify in her mind. Could he have hung around yesterday to assess her competence?

Once the seed was planted there she just couldn't shake it off. She'd re-examined every conversation they'd had. The fact he'd offered to sit with Billy to let her take Jill to the canteen. The truth was Jill hadn't eaten much at all.

But for the first time Jill had agreed to leave Billy's bedside and have a few hours' sleep in an actual bed. The NICU had two small rooms— just big cupboards, really—where parents could actually lie down and sleep, then have a shower if they wished. If Harry was examining her care, surely he could see how important it was to take care of mum too?

Billy's post-op care had been unremarkable, but when she'd read the theatre notes Esther realised just how touch and go it had been for him. Even if she'd initially detested him Harry Beaumont was a skilled surgeon, and looking at the neat clean scar line on Billy's tiny chest and the way his lungs filled with air every few moments, the scare in Theatre seemed a lifetime away.

Esther's stomach had churned as she'd made her way to the unit that day. She'd washed her hair and made sure her scrubs were immaculate. Even applying a little more make-up to her still slightly pale face. And that annoyed her too, because she'd always been immaculate at work. So why did it seem even more important that day? In a way she'd almost been annoyed when she realised Harry Beaumont wasn't there after all. But the annoyance had quickly given way to relief. On a day like today she wanted to be comfortable at work. All her concentration had to be on Billy and his mother. Not on some random, tall, dark and handsome arrogant fool with toffee-coloured eyes.

Heat rushed into her cheeks as she finished another set of Billy's checks. Where had that thought come from?

Abi nudged her elbow. 'So, anyway, I was telling you. We've found out what branch of royalty our new surgeon has.' She smiled brightly as if she thought Esther might actually be interested. 'He's from your neck of the woods. He's a duke. From Scotland. The Duke of Montrose.'

Esther wrinkled her nose. 'There's nothing

Scottish about him. Have you heard that cut-glass accent?'

Abi laughed. 'What—you don't have posh people in Scotland?'

Esther had to smile too. 'Sure we do. But not in my neck of the woods. Anyhow, when these people get titles, it doesn't mean it relates to where they stay, or where they're from. The Prince of Wales wasn't born and brought up in Wales, was he?'

Abi frowned for a second. 'I guess not.' She waved her hand as she started to walk away. 'Anyway, just thought you'd want to know.'

Esther was surprised. 'Why on earth did you think I'd want to know?'

Abi's eyebrows rose. 'Just in case you were plotting a murder. Thought you'd want to know who he is before you kill him.' She was grinning as she left, but Esther pressed her lips together.

Okay. Abi hadn't mentioned anything about the day before. But people were clearly talking. At some point she'd expect Harry to appear again and review Billy. If she were lucky, somebody else would be on duty. If not, it was really important that she didn't give off *those* vibes. The ones that said, *If I was a superhero and had powers, I'd strike you down with my laser vision.*

She had to maintain her professional composure. It didn't matter they'd had a few fallouts. The patients were the most important thing in NICU. It was important that an easy ambience was kept in place. She could be civil. She might not smile, but she could certainly be civil.

'Hey, Esther, can you take a call from Harry Beaumont? He wants a report on Billy.'

She stiffened and picked up Billy's chart. 'Sure.'

It seemed like she'd have to start right now. She picked up the phone from where it was lying on the nurses' station and did actually smile as she kept things deliberately formal. 'This is Esther McDonald, Billy's midwife, can I help you?'

There was a pause at the end of the line. 'This is Harry Beaumont, the neonatal cardiac surgeon who carried out Billy's surgery yesterday. Can you give me an update on how he's doing, please?'

Oh. It seemed that two could play that game.

The smile stayed on her face. She gave Harry a quick rundown on all of Billy's obs, new blood results, his colour and then…she did what she always did. She told him how she felt. There was something to be said about the instinct of a health professional. She always believed it should never be ignored. Sometimes, even though there was not a single piece of scientific fact, a health professional just seemed to know if a patient was going to go 'off.' So many times, their instincts had been correct. Studies had even been done on the phenomenon.

So she went with her gut. 'Billy's good. Everything is going well. I think he's on the road to recovery.'

'That's your professional opinion?' There was something in his tone. She wasn't quite sure if he was mocking her, or if he actually got it.

'I have a good feeling,' she replied.

'Okay.' His voice was thoughtful. He paused for a few seconds. 'Thanks for the update. I should be back by tomorrow. I'll review him in person then. How's his mum doing?'

Once again, Esther was a little surprised. The surgeons she'd worked with before generally didn't take the time to consider the parents. 'Sleeping,' she said. 'For the first time in days. She's taken a shower and washed her hair too. When she wakes up, I'm going to send her down to the hospital canteen with one of my colleagues to make sure she eats.'

'Does she really have no supports? Does no one else come to visit Billy?'

Esther's curiosity was piqued. Not only was he interested, he actually sounded concerned. 'Not the whole time I've been here,' she said.

'Hmm...' She could tell he was thinking. Her

brain was whirring. Maybe he wasn't quite as bad as she'd first thought.

'Esther, can I just check? Your temperature yesterday, it's resolved?'

And there it was. Just when she'd finally had a reasonable thought about this man it was like he'd just pulled the rug from under her feet.

In a way she understood the question. His issue was protecting the baby he'd operated on. But the question was intensely personal. Just as well she didn't have anything to hide.

'My temperature is resolved.'

'The reason?'

She bristled. It seemed to be her permanent state when she had any contact with this man. She couldn't remember the last time she'd felt like this about anyone. He was checking up on her—again.

She decided to put all her cards on the table. 'Don't worry. I don't have a respiratory infection.' If she had, she knew she'd have to have bailed out of the NICU for a few days. There were strict rules adhered to by all the members of staff in the NICU. 'I have a UTI,' she added. 'Long-term history, and I've got antibiotics.'

It was too much information. But she wanted this guy off her back. As a health care professional she wasn't embarrassed to talk about medical conditions. She really didn't think she had anything to hide.

There was a few moments' silence at the end of the phone, then his voice sounded deep and husky. 'I hope you feel better soon, Esther.'

She licked her lips as she put down the phone, a strange buzz going up her arm. She was feeling a little warm again. Maybe it was time for some more paracetamol?

CHAPTER FOUR

Her phone buzzed and she checked it as she walked into A&E. 'Hi, Mum, everything okay?'

She listened for a few minutes as her mum filled her in on the last few days. Her heart always twisted in her chest when her mum's name came up on her phone. It always made her wonder if it was going to be something she didn't want to hear.

Her mum had fought cancer a few years ago, the worst part being she'd initially kept it a secret from Esther because she didn't want to distract her from her studies. Esther had been absolutely devastated when she'd found out—particularly when she'd realised her mum had gone through the diagnosis and some of her treatment on her own. Guilt had overwhelmed her, that her mother had put her first in her own biggest time of need. They'd always been so close and the treatment had left her mother unable to work any more. Hence, why Esther worked every shift she could. She had to pay rent in London, which was always extortionate, plus the mortgage payment on her mum's home in Edinburgh. But there was only two years left on the mortgage. She could do it. She just had to keep up with the extra shifts.

'I'm glad you're doing okay,' said Esther, her shoulders going down a little in relief.

'Please don't work too hard, honey,' came the reply. 'I'm so sorry about all this.' This conversation happened in every call. Her mum felt massively guilty that her daughter was helping support her now.

But what else could she do? Her dad had died a few years earlier. He'd been wonderful, if a little harum-scarum. He'd drifted from job to job. Her mother had always really been the breadwinner in the household. Her father's jobs had always revolved around his passions. He'd been an extra for film companies, a body-double, had a go at training as a stunt man, then he'd taken jobs everywhere as a tour guide. He'd always seemed to like jumping from place to place, before coming home to his girls with a whole host of wonderful stories to tell.

Although they'd both loved and adored him, his attitude to work had put a strain on things for her mum, who'd counted every penny. It had ingrained in Esther the fact that security and a steady job were one of the most important things in life.

'It's fine, Mum, please don't worry. You paid the first twenty-three years, let me pay off the rest.' She spoke for another few minutes, then ended the call.

The board in A&E was full. It was going to be a busy night.

She walked down to where the shift handover normally happened. The first person she saw was Rob, the ANP. He groaned and grabbed her elbow. 'I called yesterday—didn't you get the message to call me back?'

She shook her head. He walked into one of the consulting rooms and took out a key to open a locked drawer. 'The lab work showed that the antibiotic you're on won't work this time. You need something different.'

He handed over a prescription bottle with her name on it.

She nodded. 'I wondered why I wasn't feeling better so quickly. Okay, I'll swap them over.' She opened the bottle and swallowed the first tablet with some water. 'All good.' She smiled at him.

'Are you sure?'

'Yes, now let's get to the handover.'

Thursdays were a strange day in A&E. Everyone always expected weekends to be busy, but Thursdays liked to keep staff hanging, wondering if it was going to be a lull before the storm, or a full-on tornado.

Today, the waiting room was packed.

'Where do you want me?' asked Esther.

'Can you cover cubicles?' asked the charge nurse as he tried to assign everyone to their spot.

'No trouble.' She picked up the charts for the cubicles nearby and scanned them. Stitches. A fractured wrist. A patient waiting for a bed in Respiratory. Another patient needing a catheter inserted due to urinary strictures, and a confused elderly patient that had been found wandering near one of the parks and was bordering on hypothermic. More than enough to keep her busy.

Six hours later she still hadn't had a break. Esther knew she really needed to grab some more paracetamol and another dose of her new antibiotics but she literally hadn't had a minute.

'Where's the nurse who works in NICU?' she heard a harassed voice say. 'And someone call the paed doctor?'

Esther stuck her head from behind the cubicle curtains where she'd just finished stitching up a laceration. 'I'm here. Need a hand?'

The doctor she didn't know that well nodded. 'Please, I've got a newborn who doesn't look great.'

Esther nodded. 'Absolutely.' She snapped off

the gloves she was wearing and grabbed a new pair, striding quickly alongside the doctor. She could sense his panic. And she understood it. He was new to the department and relatively junior. Dealing with babies could be scary. Paediatrics wasn't everyone's bag.

She stepped into the cubicle and saw the baby still clutched in its mother's arms. She sat down in the chair next to her. 'Hi there. I'm Esther, a midwife and a nurse. Can you tell me what happened today?'

The mother was trembling. She knew it was important to get a good history from the mother, and to try and keep things calm.

She caught a waft of something and sensed someone had come in at her back. But she kept her concentration on the baby. She really needed to get a look at either he or she.

'I h-had a home delivery last week. Everything was fine. But…he's just gone downhill fast. He's not feeding well, he keeps being sick. His colour is bad, and he gasps when he's breathing.'

Esther nodded and held out her arms towards the mother. 'Okay, sounds like I need to take a little look at him. What's his name?'

'Jude.'

She smiled and kept her hands outstretched. 'Do you mind if I take a look at Jude?'

The woman hesitated and then finally handed over the little baby. Esther moved slowly and laid the little boy down on the A&E trolley.

She knew instantly that the person on her shoulder was Harry, and after one look at this baby, for once, she wasn't too sorry he was there.

He'd walked into the cubicle just a few steps behind Esther. Paeds had received three panicked calls from A&E. He couldn't quite understand why Esther was working down here, but he gave her space to talk to what was clearly a very anxious mother. She handled the situation well and he waited until she'd moved the baby to the trolley before moving to the other side. He gave a nod to the mother and opened his mouth to speak but Esther got there first.

'Was Jude full term when he was born?'

The mum shook her head. 'Thirty-eight weeks but the midwife said there was nothing to worry about.'

Harry took his stethoscope from his neck and smiled at the mum. 'I'm Harry, I'm one of the paediatric doctors. I'm just going to check Jude over if that's okay with you.'

The woman gave an anxious nod and Harry waited patiently as Esther unwound a finger probe from the paed monitor and attached it to Jude's tiny finger.

Harry had learned not to introduce himself as a paediatric surgeon; it had a tendency to freak people out. Truth was, the paed doctor who was on call was dealing with a meningitis case in one of the wards upstairs. When Harry had heard there was a baby with potential breathing difficulties, he'd offered to cover the call.

And he was glad he had.

This little guy was using all his accessory muscles to breathe. It only took a few seconds to show that he was bradycardic, and his oxygen saturation was lower than he would have hoped for.

Esther didn't say a word, just reached for the oxygen and handed him the chart. She was efficient, he'd give her that.

She slid the nasal prongs into place and picked up an ear thermometer. Harry listened carefully to Jude's chest, hearing exactly what he expected to.

There was a definite heart defect. One he'd need to diagnose after a few more investigations. In the meantime he pulled over the sonogram without waiting for a sonographer and had a quick look for himself.

Esther was talking in a low voice to little Jude. He was responding, blinking and kicking his arms and legs. His skin was a little dusky, but not enough to cause huge concerns for Harry.

He suspected this was something he could solve with surgery in the next few days. It wasn't uncommon for heart defects not to be obvious in babies straight away. The most severe were normally picked up at prenatal scans. But the less severe could be missed.

He moved around and sat in the chair next to the mum, then paused, realising he didn't know her name.

It was like Esther read his mind. She glanced at the chart he'd left sitting on the other side of the trolley and gave a casual smile. 'Claire, Harry our doctor is going to explain what he thinks is going on with Jude right now.'

Harry gave her a grateful nod. 'Is there anyone else here with you?'

Claire shook her head, her eyes bright with tears. 'I just panicked and brought him in. I tried to phone my husband and my mum-in-law but neither of them answered. I left messages.'

Esther nodded. 'How about I have a quick check in the waiting room to see if either of them have arrived?'

Two minutes later she returned with a breathless man and an older-looking woman with her bag clutched to her chest. Both of them immediately crowded over Jude. Harry waited for them to ease their panic. The guy came and put his arm around his wife. 'What's going on?'

'He went a funny colour when he was feeding and it just didn't get better.'

The older woman was stroking Jude's head and whispering to him. It was clear Claire had supports in place that Jill in the NICU could badly do with. Harry introduced himself and shook hands, then took some time explaining what was wrong with Jude's heart, drew a diagram for them explaining how surgery would fix things.

It was clear they were horrified, but Esther was smooth, finding tissues for tears, then a chair for gran, whose legs seemed to fold once she found out her precious first grandson needed surgery.

'But who can do it?'

'I'll do it.'

'You do surgery on babies' hearts? Doesn't that need to be a specialist?'

'I am a specialist. I'm a visiting surgeon at the Queen Victoria. Cardiac surgery in babies is my speciality.'

Esther's eyes locked with his, and she gave the slightest nod of her head, as if she approved of how he was talking to the mum.

'How many times have you done this operation?'

Harry counted in his head. 'This will be number twenty-seven.'

There was an audible sigh of relief. He understood that. Esther made a few notes and stepped outside the cubicle while he kept talking to the family.

When she came back in he had just finished explaining that they'd transfer Jude upstairs and make arrangements for admission.

'Done,' said Esther, handing him the paperwork. 'Porter is just coming. Francesca will review Jude on the ward.'

Harry raised his eyebrows. 'You don't waste time.'

She gave him a tight smile. 'Some people call me efficient.'

He shifted on his feet. Was she mad at him again? He thought they'd sorted things. The porter arrived quickly and Harry decided to head up to the ward with the family.

He booked the theatre time for the next day and spoke to Francesca before heading back down to A&E. It only took him a few minutes to find Esther again. She was clearing up a tray of bloody swabs.

'Whoa.'

She looked up. ''Gunshot wound. Thankfully it was just a graze.'

'Do midwives normally treat gunshot wounds?'

She blinked. 'I'm a nurse too. That's why I

get to work in A&E.' She paused for a second and then added, 'How's your baby in France?'

He pulled a face. 'Post-op complications. He developed a pulmonary embolism. Probably not much bigger than the head of pin. But in a twenty-five-weeker...'

He looked up and realised she was holding her breath. 'Oh, everything's good now. We're back to a "wait and see."'

'How come you were down covering?'

'I'd just got back from France and came in to check on Billy. I'd gone along to the ward and saw the messages about the A&E referral. The doc in Paeds was dealing with a meningitis case so I offered to cover.'

'That was nice of you.' Her eyebrows were raised.

'What? You don't think I can be nice?'

She tilted her head to the side. 'To be honest, I don't know what I think of you, Harry Beaumont, or should I call you the Duke of Montrose?'

He winced. His title followed him everywhere. Not that he ever really used it. Only at family occasions when he had to.

Her hand went to her mouth to cover a yawn, and he was instantly suspicious.

'Excuse me,' she said as she dug her hand into

her pocket and pulled out some antibiotics, tipping one out and swallowing it.

'You're still not feeling better?' They were under the bright lights of the treatment room and it struck him that she pretty much looked like when he'd seen her on that first day.

She gave a half-hearted shrug. 'They've changed my antibiotics. I was resistant to the first lot and I didn't get the message until today.'

'So, you still have a temp and feel knackered?'

She spun towards him in surprise. 'Since when did you get all Scottish?' She let out a little laugh. 'Have you any idea how that word sounds in an accent like yours?'

He grinned at her. 'Does it sound any better when I say Crabbie Rabbie?'

She crossed her arms in front of her chest. 'Right, that's it. It's official. You're banned from saying that. In fact—' she headed to the door of the treatment room '—you're banned from any Scottish words.' She shot him a teasing glance. 'I'm not buying the Duke of Montrose title. You're about as Scottish as the London subway.'

He opened his mouth in pretend horror. 'Esther McDonald, are you mocking me?'

She gave a shake of her head. 'Oh, Harry, I haven't even started yet.'

She started to walk away, 'Sorry, got to run. Busy.'

* * *

Things just got crazier. And Esther got more and more tired by the second. Could there be a chance the second set of antibiotics weren't right for her either? That would definitely be unusual. Plus it would start to freak her out that she might have an infection that was multiresistant. That had never happened to her before, and she knew they could be serious.

The more tired she got, the more patients crowded through the door. She spent time with a young woman who came in with symptoms of pregnancy that she clearly was ignoring. She kept refusing to accept she was pregnant and her behaviour got more and more erratic. Eventually Esther realised she needed someone other than the A&E docs to assess this young lady. She called one of the psychiatric liaison nurses who was able to discover that their patient had a pre-existing mental-health condition and had in fact realised she was pregnant, and had stopped her regular medication in case it caused harm to her baby. Now, her condition was spiralling and she needed some help.

Next up was an elderly lady who'd fallen and broken her hip, lying on the ground for a few hours before she was found. Hypothermia was setting in, and Esther had to try and get her warmed up in the first instance before she could even be assessed for potential surgery.

As the evening progressed Esther started to develop an unconscious itch. She couldn't understand it. It started on her back, then moved to her abdomen. She was monitoring her lady's temperature for the fifth time when Harry caught her standing on one of the corners of the department using the wall edge to scratch her back.

He stopped walking and looked at her. 'Esther, have you looked in the mirror lately?'

'Do I look as if I've had time to look in a mirror lately?' It was snappier than she meant it to be.

He put his hands firmly on her shoulders and walked her across the corridor to the accessible toilet that had a large mirror on the wall. He flicked on the light and she gasped.

Red blotches stared at her, climbing all the way up her neck. 'Oh my…' Propriety was out the window. She pulled up her scrub top and looked at her abdomen. Yip. Covered, along with a whole host of scratch marks. She lifted her scrub top at the back. 'Can you check my back?'

She wasn't the least embarrassed to ask. He was a doctor, and he was right there.

He bent down and took a look, just in time for one of the other A&E members of staff to walk by and raise their eyebrows. Thankfully Harry didn't notice as he stood up and shook his head. 'You're covered.' His finger touched the top of her arm where her scrub top ended. 'Look, they're starting to appear on your arms too.'

She looked down; sure enough, a red, angry-looking blotch was only half hidden by the sleeve of her scrub top.

'No wonder I've been so itchy.' She sighed. She'd been so busy she hadn't had time to stop and think about it.

'New body lotion? New washing powder?' he asked.

She shook her head. 'No, nothing.' Then something lined up in her brain. 'Oh, darn it.' She reached into her scrub top and pulled out her pill bottle. 'These antibiotics. I've never had these before. It must be them.'

Before she had a chance to say anything else Harry reached over and wrapped his hand around her wrist. She didn't get a chance to object as he led her down the corridor to the treatment room. He stuck his head back out. 'Rob!' His shout was loud and commanding, and a few seconds later Rob the ANP appeared.

'Do you have the key for the medicine trolley?' Harry asked as Esther let out a few coughs.

Rob frowned, glancing from Harry to Esther,

his eyes narrowing as he looked at her. He pulled the keys from his pocket. 'Yes.'

Harry held out his hand. 'I think she's having an allergic reaction to those new antibiotics. I'm going to give her some antihistamines.'

Rob moved over, touching her face and turning it from side to side to check either side of her neck. 'Any wheezing? Difficulty breathing?'

She shook her head but let out another cough.

'How bad is the rash?' he asked. She sighed and partly lifted her scrub top again, letting Rob bend down to have a quick check.

'Darn it,' he said. 'I'm going to record this in your notes and get you something else.'

Harry named another antibiotic. 'Try that one,' he said to Rob as he opened a bottle of tablets and tipped two into Esther's hand.

Esther turned on the tap and swallowed the antihistamines with a little water in a medicine cup. This rash was getting itchier by the second.

Okay, she'd been itchy earlier. But she knew this was psychological. Now she'd seen it and realised it was there, she just wanted to claw at herself. Lovely.

Harry had a worried look on his face, and she wasn't sure whether to feel grateful, or a bit annoyed. She put her hand on the worktop in the treatment room for a second as a wave of tiredness hit her.

She calculated in her head how many days she'd been fighting this infection now. The tiredness had still been there but she'd tried her best to ignore it, believing as soon as the antibiotics kicked in, it would just lift. That's what had always happened in the past.

'I have to go back and check obs on my woman,' she said to Harry. 'Thanks for the help. I guess I'll see you later.'

'You can't go out there looking like that. And wait until Rob comes back with some new antibiotics. I think you should sit down for a while.'

Her face went automatically into a frown and he held up both hands. 'Not trying to tell you what to do.' His mouth started to form other words and she thought for a second he was going to use her nickname, but he smiled, must have thought better of it and stopped. 'But have you had a break today?'

She shook her head. 'Then what about a coffee? Even in the staff room for five minutes? Let Rob write up his paperwork and come back with something.'

The thought of sitting down for five minutes was tempting. 'But what about my patient?'

'Cubicle five?'

She nodded.

'Let me tell the charge nurse you need a five-minute break and ask if someone else can check on your lady.' Harry pulled a face. 'I hate to break it to you, Esther, but you are actually having an allergic reaction to antibiotics. It's quite severe. Let's just be sure it doesn't progress. Let's be safe.'

It was the way he said those words. She was so much of the 'drag yourself into work no matter what' mentality—one that a lot of nurses had—that she never really stopped and took time for herself. The truth was, with the extra hours she'd been doing, she hadn't had any time. Would five minutes really matter? She should have been sent for a break a few hours ago.

'Okay,' she said reluctantly.

Harry nodded and walked down the corridor in long strides. Esther made her way to the staff room and flicked the switch on the kettle.

There was a huge box of cupcakes and doughnuts in the middle of the table from a bakery that was quite exclusive. Anything left in the staff room was pretty much a free-for-all and she was surprised there were any left.

As she took down a couple of cups Harry came back through the door. 'All sorted. I told Rob where we are and he's just finished the paperwork.'

Where *we* are. She wasn't quite sure how she felt about that phrase.

She turned back. 'Does that mean you're planning on hanging around?'

He nodded. 'I'm monitoring your reaction.'

As soon as he said those words she scratched again.

'Whilst eating cakes,' he added.

She spooned coffee into two cups and filled them with boiling water. It would be rude not to, but she didn't plan on being too hospitable. 'Milk's in the fridge if you want it,' she said as she handed over the cup.

He stood quickly to get some. 'Don't you want some?' he asked as he added milk to his cup.

She smiled. 'No, not here. I never trust milk dates when I'm in the hospital. I always drink my coffee black in here.'

He stared suspiciously into his cup as he sat back down. 'Yeah, thanks for that.' He pushed the box towards her. 'Eat something.'

'I wonder where these came from?' she asked as a strawberry cupcake seemed to shout her name.

'Me,' he said.

'You brought cakes to A&E? You didn't even know you'd be down here.'

He gave her a calculating smile. 'I brought multiple boxes. I left one in NICU, one in Paeds and one down here.'

'Trying to win people around because occasionally you can be a bit brusque?'

He lifted a chocolate doughnut and met her gaze. There was something quite electric about those eyes. She was glad she was sitting, because the look would likely have stopped her in her tracks. 'Has anyone ever told you that you speak your mind?'

She laughed. 'No. Why would anyone ever tell me that?' She nibbled at the cupcake. 'But let me warn you, you think I'm bad? Try meeting Oona our charge nurse. If you think I was smart about the entourage, she would have chewed you up and spat you out.'

'Nice.' He nodded. 'Okay, then, if this is a teaching hospital, exactly how many am I allowed to bring in to NICU?'

'Students?'

He nodded.

'Two. And they better follow the infection control procedures. To the letter.'

He leaned over and gently slapped her hand. 'Stop scratching.'

He was right. She was clawing away at her neck again and hadn't even noticed. 'When are these antihistamines going to start to kick in?' She let out a long, exhausted breath.

Harry glanced at his watch. 'Probably not for another hour at least.'

Now she'd sat down, tiredness was really starting to overwhelm her, and it didn't matter how nice Harry had been to her today, because of their altercation a few days before, the last thing she wanted to do was show him just how tired she was at work. Not when she had patients to see, and other staff relying on her.

But Harry was being nice to her. She couldn't pretend anything else. Today, he'd given her space to deal with the mother and baby. Not all doctors were like that. Some would just have barged in and taken over.

The truth was, she was slightly curious about him. He must have worked hard to gain his position as a neonatal cardiac surgeon. As for the duke stuff? He certainly hadn't told anyone his title, but information like that was quick to follow a person.

She was suddenly conscious they were the only people in the room, and even though she was at the other side of the coffee table, his fresh scent was drifting over towards her. When she was feeling as tired and woozy as this, it was kind of hypnotic. She felt as if she had to get out of here.

She pushed herself up. 'I better get back. I have another hour before I'm off shift. You've seen it out there, it's chaos. I can't stay here eating cakes.'

She'd made it to the door by then, but Harry was right alongside her, his fingers brushing her arm. 'Even if you're sick?'

She licked her lips. She couldn't pretend she felt one hundred per cent. She was feeling hot again, and she wanted to find Rob and get started on the third set of antibiotics. No wonder her body felt so tired from constantly fighting an infection.

She gave him a tight smile. 'You know how the health service is.' She ducked out the door before Harry had a chance to say anything else, his fingers burning an imprint on her skin.

She didn't finish her shift an hour later. Harry knew, because after reviewing Billy in NICU, and making arrangements for the new baby's surgery, his feet just seemed to automatically take him back downstairs to A&E to check on her.

It was crazy. He didn't even understand it himself. But there was something about this occasionally angry Scottish midwife that was just pulling him in.

He was quite sure she didn't want him there. But even though they'd had a bad start, he'd watched her interactions with others, with patients, and the respect she had from other staff, and all of it intrigued him.

So he stood in the corridor as he watched her dash back and forward between cubicles. Rob came and stood alongside him, folding his arms and leaning against the wall like Harry, mirroring his stance.

'Are you doing what I think you're doing?'

'Her rash seems to have died down a bit, but shouldn't she have gone home by now?' He turned towards Rob. 'Shouldn't you have gone home too?'

Rob shrugged. 'You know how it is.' His eyes went to Esther, who hadn't noticed either of them as she stopped for a second in the corridor and put her hand on the wall. She looked absolutely exhausted.

They shot each other a glance and walked over to her. 'Okay,' Rob said quickly. 'Esther, I'm officially sending you home. I should have done it earlier, but to be truthful I thought you would have responded much quicker to the antihistamines. I'm sorry.'

'But my patients…'

Rob interrupted her. 'They'll be reassigned.'

She sagged a little as relief clearly flooded over her. 'Great.'

He tilted his head and looked at her again. 'Is there someone at home with you?'

She scowled. 'No. Why?'

Rob bit his bottom lip. 'I actually wonder if I

should make you stay overnight in the combined assessment unit—you know, for observation?'

He was glancing at Harry again.

She shook her head fiercely. 'No way. Not a chance.'

'Esther, I'm not sure I should let you go home. What if something happens in the middle of the night? What if you feel unwell? How will you get back in?'

Esther gave Harry a look of panic. The dark circles under her eyes pulled at something inside him.

No member of NHS staff wanted to see a colleague look like this.

Harry stood for a few moments next to her, not wanting to leave. It was a strange sensation for him. A few days ago he'd been ready to do battle with this midwife, questioning her competence. But here she was, working in A&E as well as NICU. There had to be a story there, and he was curious what it was. Now he'd seen her working, he knew she was dedicated. He just didn't know why she was taking on so many shifts to the detriment of her own health. He might not be an expert, he might not even know her that well, but from what little he'd seen, Esther was on the verge of burnout.

She gave a soft smile, and shook her head again. He could tell she was going to try and persuade Rob to let her go. She gave an unconscious scratch of her neck and gave Harry a sad kind of smile. 'Thanks for looking out for me earlier.'

'Of course.' He meant it. He'd look out for any member of staff that was clearly unwell at work.

He held up his hand. 'Stay here. Both of you. Don't move.'

There was a phone on the nearby wall and he picked it up, calling up to first NICU, then the paed ward. Everything appeared to be under control. The other doc on call was more than competent. 'Head home, Harry. Anything happens with your own patients I've got your mobile and I'll give you a call. But you can trust me, you know?' he added in a jokey tone.

'Okay.' Harry hung up the phone. He had to get better at that. Trusting others with his patients. Maybe it was because he'd spent so long being the visiting expert surgeon. It meant he couldn't form relationships long enough with people to feel assured about their competencies.

Or maybe it was because of the way he'd been brought up. No child asked to be born to parents who weren't the least bit interested in them. A child had been a necessity for the duke and duchess. Someone to carry on the family name. But that's all he'd been. It had taken him a long time to realise that the relationship he had with his parents wasn't entirely normal. Most kids who boarded did actually get to spend some time at home. But not Harry. It made forming relationships hard for him. He'd spent most of his childhood thinking he didn't deserve love, and most of his wild teenage years looking for love wherever he could find it. Medicine had been his blessing. His focus. Surgery his ultimate goal. He'd managed to keep everything right on track until the death of his father had derailed one of his first surgeries.

He'd had to leave. It was unheard of for a son not to attend his father's funeral. The gossip columns would have loved it. His mother had died years previously, so he was the only family left to make the arrangements. So, only two days after his first neonatal cardiac surgery, he'd had to travel home for the funeral.

He'd had to leave the tiny baby he'd wanted to watch like a hawk. And it had happened. The death. While he wasn't there. His first experience of a child death review with his name as the surgeon. It was devastating for him, and had almost derailed his career. He would never know if something else could have been done to save that baby. None of them would. But it had left an indelible mark on Harry. One he couldn't ever shake off, or forget.

These babies were his responsibility and he

could never forget that. Working with a hundred different teams across a variety of continents was difficult for him. Being a visiting surgeon was hard.

Some weeks he didn't even get to sleep in his own bed. Constantly moving from place to place—sometimes from country to country to perform his specialist kind of surgery. At first he'd liked it. Enjoyed it even.

But constantly working with different staff was wearing. He'd never considered it before, but the thought of having his own team—a team that he would train by himself and he could trust—had started to play on his mind.

He could also get to know all the staff who worked in NICU and Paeds and perhaps even have a little confidence in the people around him. He could actually start to get a life again—or even get to spend some time in his own bed, in his own home. Now that would really be a miracle.

He walked back over, the decision already made in his head. 'Okay, Esther. You're coming home with me.'

'What?' She looked entirely stunned.

He shrugged. 'This is easy. You have two choices. You let Rob admit you, or you let me take you home and keep an eye on you overnight.'

She opened her mouth to speak but he kept talking.

'I know what's happened. I know the history. I'm not going to tell anyone else, and you don't need to tell anyone you stayed with me. If you're unwell during the night I can bring you back in.'

The stunned look hadn't changed. Harry's conscience was tugging at heartstrings he didn't even know he had. But every cell in his body told him this was the right thing to do.

Rob shot him a glance and a nod. He folded his arms across his chest. 'Sounds good to me, but it's entirely your choice, Esther. I think you need supervision for at least the next eight hours. Where you spend them is up to you.'

She shot them both a look of complete exasperation. 'Fine, fine.' She threw up her hands. 'Just let me go and get changed.'

She turned and walked off to the female changing room. Harry went into the other changing room and stowed his white coat and pulled out his jacket. He was still waiting to be allocated an office. Hospital space was always tight, so until then, he was happy to have somewhere safe to leave his things.

As he pulled his car keys from his trouser pocket he saw Esther standing at the exit to A&E. Her head was turning from side to side as if she were contemplating the option to run. The weather had turned and rain was bucketing down.

He moved outside, his shoulder brushing against hers. The sun was setting in the sky, sending purple streaks above them.

Harry didn't hesitate. 'Your place or mine?'

He could see something flit across her face. 'Why are you doing this?' Her voice was quiet, almost a whisper.

He'd asked himself the same question. 'Because I should,' he said simply. 'It's the right thing to do.'

There was a long pause, then Esther's shoulders sagged a little, just like they had earlier, as if she'd accepted that answer. 'It will take too long to get to mine. You must be tired. I'm sure you stay closer.' She was saying the words but he could see something else in her eyes. Maybe she didn't want him to see where she lived?

'You're sure about this?' she repeated, her hand gripping tightly to the handle of her bag.

'I'm sure. Come on.' He started walking across the car park, pressing the buttons on his remote to open the doors. 'Relax,' he laughed over his shoulder. 'You're acting like I'm kidnapping you. Rob knows I've taken you home.

If you're never seen again, he'll send the police after me.'

'Oh, reassure me, why don't you,' she quipped back.

As they reached the car she stopped walking and looked at him, eyebrow slightly arched, as the rain thudded around them. 'Really?'

He shrugged. 'What? Excessive?'

She opened the door to the dark blue Aston Martin and climbed in. As he slid in beside her she shook her head. 'No, excessive would have been a royal carriage. And at this point in the day, I'd go home in anything.'

She leaned back into the seat. 'Should I call you James Bond, instead of Duke?'

He smiled at her teasing. 'Harry will be fine, thanks.' He started the engine. 'I think I told you before I'm not far from here. Where do you live?'

'Dagenham, not the same as you in Belgravia.' The edges of her lips curled upwards.

He gave a nod and pulled out of the car park. No wonder she was tired. The tube between the Queen Victoria and Dagenham would add almost an hour each way onto her journey every day.

He waited until they were in the traffic before he glanced towards her. 'So, how come you work so much?'

Her eyes were already halfway closed. She let out a sigh. 'My mum needs some help back home. She's had cancer and although she's in remission the chemo and radiotherapy meant she's never got back to full fitness and can't get back to work.' She turned her head. 'I need to cover the mortgage. It's only got a couple of years left. I can do it.'

The words came out in a stream and he knew if she hadn't been half as exhausted she probably wouldn't have told him any of this.

His head was immediately filled with a barrage of questions that it wasn't good manners to ask. At least now he understood. She had a real reason to work every hour there was. She obviously felt responsible for her mum.

Something twisted in his gut. Even those few words let him know that Esther and her mother had a real bond, a real connection. He shifted in his seat uncomfortably. He'd never known what that felt like. His parents had always been like distant ornaments sitting on a grand mantelpiece.

He'd spent more happy years at boarding school, and at university, than he ever had being back in their grand estate. Taking ownership of the Belgravia town house had felt like a huge sigh of relief that he wouldn't be expected to be under the same roof as them for any length of time.

Esther's eyes were fully closed and her breathing steady. She was fast asleep and they'd barely been in the car a few minutes.

Her dark hair was coming loose from its braid and for a few moments his eyes fixated on her long dark lashes. How had he not really noticed them before?

The car behind him beeped and he moved the Aston Martin quickly through the traffic, letting some quiet music play in the background as they drove.

Esther remained fast asleep. He could still see the edge of some of the rash at the bottom of her neck. The steroids should have kicked in a few hours before. Her reaction had obviously been a bit more serious than any one of them had realised.

By the time he'd pulled into the parking for his town house, his initial confidence had waned a little. He switched off the engine and walked around to her side of the car. The lift in the converted basement could take him right up to the top floor of the town house, where the bedrooms were.

He opened the door, and paused again to see if she would wake. Nothing. 'Esther,' he said gently. 'I'm just going to pick you up.'

She murmured something in reply. It didn't sound like a no, so he slid his arms under her and picked her up, grabbing her bag and closing the car door with his hip.

The lift took them upstairs in seconds and he flicked on a light with his elbow, and walked down the corridor towards one of the empty bedrooms in his house.

They were all beautifully decorated, fresh and light. He laid her down on top of one of the beds, then slid off her shoes. He didn't want her to panic if she woke up, so when he closed the heavy curtains, he turned the bedside light on, setting it to dim.

The en suite bathroom was stocked with supplies. She could find anything she might need in here. Her jacket pocket jangled as he slid it from her shoulders. Of course. Her new antibiotics. He couldn't let her go without them.

He sat the antibiotics on the table and saw that Rob had added in a couple of extra antihistamines. Harry grabbed her a glass of water from the bathroom and sat out the pills she needed to take.

He spoke as gently as he could. 'Esther, you need to take your antibiotics, and another antihistamine. You still have a bit of a reaction going on. Can you take these for me?' He pressed them into one hand and held the glass in his other.

Something must have clicked in her brain. She didn't open her eyes, but put the tablets in her mouth. Harry closed her hand around the glass of water and her body acted automatically, lifting the glass to her mouth and swallowing. The second it was done she hunkered back down into the bed, lying on her side.

Harry pulled a pale yellow blanket up from the bottom of the bed. She wasn't actually under the duvet, as putting her there seemed intrusive, so he refilled her glass of water and tucked the blanket around her.

At the last moment, he scribbled a note on the pad next to her bed before he walked out and closed the door.

He'd check on her again in a few hours.

He smiled, remembering words he'd heard her say to someone else earlier that day. Something about having their head in their hands to play with if they didn't do what they were told.

It seemed highly likely that tomorrow that person would be him.

But Harry wasn't scared. In fact, he liked it.

CHAPTER FIVE

SHE HADN'T FELT this rested and comfortable in a long time. There was the warmest feeling around her, almost as if she were sleeping in some kind of luxury cocoon.

She sniffed. And that little action woke her up. A slight hint of lemon. Her flat did not smell of lemon. No matter how many air fresheners she bought. Her flat always had an underlying odour of damp.

She sat bolt upright, eyes widening at the pale yellow walls, unfamiliar furniture and the space in the room. She felt like Dorothy, waking up in a place that certainly wasn't Kansas.

There. At the bottom of the bed was a tray, with a large teapot, a slight trail of steam coming from the spout. A china cup and saucer sat next to it, along with a milk jug and small plate containing slices of lemon. That's where the smell was coming from.

Her mouth felt yucky. And she swung her legs

off the bed as she tried to make sense of things in her head. She should be shouting. She should be screaming. But she had the oddest sensation of not being gripped by panic. It was just as if her brain was playing catch up.

There, sitting on the bedside table, was her bottle of antibiotics along with a glass of water. She took one automatically and walked through to the bathroom. Her reflection in the mirror wasn't pleasant. But the accessories sitting around the white sink and vanity unit were strangely welcoming.

Her head was starting to unfog. The shift last night in A&E. How busy it was. She unconsciously scratched at her skin. She walked back and picked up the antibiotics again. Of course. These were new.

She patted herself. She still had on all her clothes. The only things removed were her jacket and her shoes, and even from here she could see these sitting clearly on a high-backed chair in the room.

Realisation struck. Harry. She'd agreed to go home with Harry. They'd got in the car together but she had absolutely no memory at all of getting here. She let out a groan. She'd fallen asleep, hadn't she?

Heat rushed into her cheeks. He must have

carried her up the stairs. Just how strong was Duke Harry?

She licked her lips and poured herself some tea. She wasn't exactly in a rush to go and find him. One glance at her watch showed her how early it was. She had time to shower, and use some of the products in the bathroom to tidy herself up. She walked over to the window and pulled back the heavy drapes.

Wow. Her fingers caught on the obviously expensive material. She ran her fingers over it a few times before hauling the curtains backwards. The road outside was peaceful; she peered downwards through the checker-paned windows at the luxury cars parked in the street outside. The house seemed to be in some kind of square. She gave a shudder, not even wanting to take a guess at what a place like this cost.

She sipped at the tea, and turned on the shower, slipping out of her clothes and putting on the cosy white dressing gown that was hanging handily behind the bathroom door. With her hair tied up on top of her head it only took a few moments for her to start waking up once she'd stepped in the steaming hot shower. Once she'd scrubbed herself dry and used the rose-scented toiletries she felt a little better. The ugly rash from last night had all but vanished. She brushed her teeth and walked back through to pull her clothes back on. But something made her hesitate. Pulling on yesterday's clothes seemed a little unpleasant. Her hand hovered next to the door. The guy had carried her upstairs and put her to bed. Would it really be so wrong to ask for a T-shirt?

As soon as she opened the door she could smell food cooking.

Her feet took her down a plush-carpeted corridor, a small set of stairs and into a white shiny kitchen. The kind normally found in a new show home that looked untouched.

Harry was in the middle of this kitchen with fresh toast, and mixing up some scrambled eggs. 'Oh, Esther, are you okay? How are you feeling?'

She moved over towards the island in the kitchen, perching on one of the stools as she watched him cook. He seemed pretty relaxed. He obviously didn't feel awkward about last night and she was thankful. This could have been a really uncomfortable morning.

She leaned her head on one hand. 'I'm sorry. I must have zonked out on you last night.'

He gave her a wary glance as he tipped the scrambled eggs onto two plates. 'That's okay. How are you feeling this morning?'

'Okay, I think. I don't have the intense itch

that I remember from last night. But there is something else.'

'Yeah? What?' His eyebrows rose as he looked at her quizzically.

She smiled. 'I'm just waiting to see if you're going to sue me for back injuries.'

He laughed and pushed the toast across the counter towards her. 'Here. Eat up. You must be starving.'

She nodded in agreement. 'Yip. I am. I missed out on the beans I was going home to last night.' She buttered her toast and took a spoonful of scrambled eggs. 'Wow. You can actually cook.'

He sat down opposite her and picked up a cafetière of coffee. 'Want some of this?'

She nodded as he poured. 'Why are you being so nice to me?'

'I am?' He fixed his dark eyes on her. It was clear he'd not long showered. The tips of his ruffled hair were still damp. When he smiled he had little crinkles around his eyes. Ones that were still there when he stopped. Obviously Harry usually smiled a lot, just not generally around her.

'Yes.' She nodded. 'You are.'

Something flashed into her brain. Something she'd told him last night. She automatically straightened in her seat. 'You felt sorry for me.'

He looked up from stirring his coffee. 'What?'

'Last night. I told you something I shouldn't have. You felt sorry for me.' She wanted to stand up and walk away. Every cell of her body was in defence mode right now.

His spoon paused just as he went to set it down. 'I didn't do this because I felt sorry for you, Esther. I did it because you were a colleague, and I was worried about you. You were clearly—' his lips turned into a smile '—knackered. And you'd had a reaction to your antibiotic. I was just looking out for you. Not—' he shook his head '—feeling sorry for you.'

She couldn't help but smile back at his use of one of her frequently used words.

She wriggled her shoulders a bit—almost as if she were trying to shake off some of her anxieties.

'How's your rash?'

She raised her eyebrows. 'Oh, so we're getting personal now?'

He wrinkled his nose in amusement. 'Well, I've seen part of your body now anyway. Is it gone?'

She shook her head at him. 'Seems to be.'

'So, no reaction to the new set of antibiotics, then?'

'Thankfully not. Don't want to end up Ms Antiresistant. That would be a disaster.'

'You said you were prone to these infections?'

She nodded. Some might find the question intrusive. But Esther wasn't like that.

'Yeah. Kidney issues as a kid means that if I'm ever a bit run-down I tend to get a flare-up. Usually I notice the symptoms quickly and get things sorted out. But I was late to notice this time around. I've been too busy working and I've never had a reaction to antibiotics before.'

'Any idea what could have caused it? Anything changed? Medical condition?' She could tell he was running through a whole host of things in his head. His eyes met hers. 'Pregnancy?'

She laughed. 'That would require a partner,' she said bluntly. 'So, not a possibility.' Her skin tingled. Had Harry actually meant to ask that question?

'So, no other half?'

Yip. He obviously had. If she didn't know better she'd say there had just been an explosion of butterflies in her stomach.

'Maybe I'm just too crabbie?' she said, half joking.

'Or maybe you're just picky,' he said, giving her an easy get-out clause.

'Don't you have a duchess stashed away somewhere?' she asked. 'Should I expect some lady in satin to walk down the corridor any second now?'

She hated how much she really didn't want that to happen. Up until this point she hadn't thought to ask the question. Now she really, really wanted to know the answer.

A slow smile spread across Harry's face. As if he could see into her curious mind right now. He waved a hand ever so casually. 'There's no duchess. No other half. Quite frankly, I haven't had the time. I'm never in one place for any length of time to even form a friendship, let alone a relationship.'

Something flitted across his face as he said that, and she immediately knew there was a whole load more to that story.

'So, as our new visiting surgeon…' She let the words trail off for a moment.

He took a sip of his coffee. His eyes stayed steadily fixed on hers. 'Yes?'

'How long you going to be visiting?' She knew her tone was teasing.

He smiled. 'Depends how nice the staff are.'

Esther put down her knife and fork. The scrambled eggs had been delicious, but they were gone now. One of her fingers twiddled with a loose piece of her hair. 'So, in my experience, what generally happens when you start working at a new place is you come in and introduce yourself to the staff and be nice to people.'

'I wasn't?' He'd raised his eyebrows. His tone was teasing too.

Esther shook her head. 'You were a rat bag and you know it.'

He laughed out loud.

'Maybe I should call you Flash Harry. In and out of the unit, after you bandy about your title and wreak havoc.'

He rolled his eyes. 'Flash Harry, like I've never heard that before.' Then he grinned. 'I like Crabbie Rabbie better.'

She shook her head. 'Will you do many surgeries at the Queen Victoria?'

She was probing. She knew she was. But the truth was, she did actually want to know how often Harry was likely to be around.

Some might say he was being mildly flirtatious with her. She wanted to know if she should be flirtatious back. She wasn't interested in anything permanent. She didn't have time for that. She couldn't even remember the last time she'd been on a date or had any downtime because she spent so much time doing extra shifts. Maybe it was time to open herself to the possibility of a little bit of fun?

Harry was watching her carefully. 'I might do a few. The theatre equipment at the Queen Victoria is brand new. I've been guaranteed theatre time for any baby affected across four counties.' He wrinkled his nose. 'If I was guessing, I'd imagine that could be around six babies a year for me.'

She gave a little smile. An occasional guest. That's how she could term him. Not around enough to interfere with her life. But maybe a familiar enough face to have a little fun with.

He licked his lips. 'It just so happens that for the next little while I'll have a few babies scheduled for surgery in the Queen Victoria. It always happens like that. So, I might be around for the next few weeks.'

The next few weeks. It could almost be music to her ears.

He closed his eyes for a second. Then he opened one and squinted at her. 'You might need to get used to me. If you'd known that at first, would we still have fought?'

She gave a thoughtful nod. 'Oh, I think so,' she said slowly, her lips curling up in a smile. She said her words with an even more teasing tone than before. 'That just seemed inevitable.'

His hand reached across the table, as if he were actually going to touch her fingers. But then it stopped midway, as if his brain had thought better of it.

His voice was low, continuing with the mutual teasing. It was like they were scoping each other out. 'Some people say that opposites attract.' The words sounded like a question.

What had seemed like an explosion of butterflies in her stomach now turned into a firework explosion in her brain.

But not in a good way. Not the way it should.

He knew they were opposites. He'd asked where she lived and she'd told him. As a man who'd probably lived in London all his life, she imagined he knew exactly what her home area was like in comparison to his. But was that what Harry was talking about? Was he talking wealth and prestige? Meaning that Esther was obviously poverty-stricken and not from an upper-class family like his?

That burned somewhere deep inside. And not in any way she liked.

'Those kind of things generally don't work out,' she said flatly. She pushed herself up from the chair. All of a sudden she wanted to get of here. She didn't need to see this luxury town house with furnishings and decor she could only dream about. There were probably paintings or chairs in this place that were worth more than the value of the flat she was currently renting.

She realised she might be being rude. It didn't matter that for a few moments she could have sworn there was some electricity in the air between them, and the fact it seemed to have disappeared in a flash was leaving a heavy feeling in the pit of her stomach.

'Thanks for looking after me last night,' she said quickly. 'But I should go now.' She looked down for a second and remembered she didn't have anything clean to put on. Would second-day clothes really be so bad?

But her second-day clothes were things that she'd slept in all night. Underwear she'd been wearing since yesterday morning.

'Don't suppose I could borrow something to put on?'

Harry's face had fallen a little as she'd spoken a few moments ago and her new words made him perk up. 'You want my clothes?'

She gave a shrug. 'Why not? I've never worn a Bond Street tailored shirt. I'm not entirely sure I'd suit it.' She let out a little laugh. 'But if you had a T-shirt and some joggies I'd be delighted. I promise to wash them and give them back. I won't hold them hostage.'

He stood up. 'Come with me, then.'

She followed him up the stairs and back along the corridor before she realised he was actually taking her to his bedroom. As they stepped inside she held in the gasp. The room was enormous. Pale green, but bright and sunny.

Whilst the decor was pleasant, her eyes went immediately to the bed that seemed bigger than any she'd seen before. It was made, which was a revelation. Most of the male friends she knew climbed out of a bed in the morning, and back into a bed at night, without doing the stuff in between. The straightening and smoothing down of the sheets and duvet.

He opened the biggest walk-in wardrobe she'd ever seen. She couldn't help but mutter, 'It's actually criminal that a guy should have this.'

He laughed and glanced over his shoulder. 'Esther McDonald, are you being sexist?'

'Of course not.' She wandered up and down. There was surprisingly a small amount of clothes in here. She could see a number of impeccable suits hanging up, polished shoes on a rack on the wall and tailored shirts lined up by colour. But the whole space was maybe only a quarter full.

'Tell me you do own some T-shirts,' she said, glancing around.

He nodded and pulled open a drawer. There they were, all neatly lined up.

She sighed. 'Harry, do you actually do all this yourself?'

He shook his head. 'Of course I don't. I spend so many hours flying between hospitals and consulting on cases I couldn't even tell you how to work the washing machine. Let alone have time to stack everything neatly.'

She folded her arms across her chest and leaned against the wall. 'Oh, how the other half live.' She said it in joking terms, but it felt like yet another divide for her. Showing just how far apart they were.

He pulled out a pair of grey joggers and a white T-shirt. 'What about these?'

'Perfect,' she said as she reached out to grab them. The soft feel of the T-shirt made her want to quickly look at the label. But she resisted the temptation.

Harry stopped above another drawer and hesitated. 'This could be a bad question.'

'Could it?' Her brow wrinkled. What was he going to ask? She shook her head. 'We've already done the falling-out part, so just ask away.'

'Do you want some socks and some underwear?'

She burst out laughing, and once she'd started she couldn't really stop.

Harry looked a bit panicked. 'Okay, was it a bad question?'

She shook her head and wiped her eyes. 'No, but I'm so wishing the shoe was on the other foot right now, and it was me, asking you, if you wanted a loan of underwear.'

He started laughing too. 'Now that *would* be interesting. I love to think what you'd offer me.'

'Don't get too excited. You might be sadly disappointed.'

There was a twinkle in his eyes. 'Oh, I doubt it.'

There it was again. The buzz she thought she might have imagined earlier. Nope. She definitely wasn't imagining this.

His phone rang and he pulled it from his pocket. She leaned against the wall and listened while he rattled out the biggest list of instructions ever for a baby that was in another unit somewhere. Something flashed in her brain and she remembered hearing Harry speak to someone a few days ago about the same baby. His face was serious, almost twisted, while he spoke, and she hated the deep furrows that had formed on his brow. She'd been offended by the way he'd spoken to her previously—even though she might not have made the best impression by sleeping in the canteen. Now, she was realising that this was how he spoke to everyone looking after the babies he termed as 'his.' She folded her arms and shook her head as he finished the call and put the phone back in his pocket.

He saw her glance and attempted to change his demeanour. 'Where were we?'

She shook her head. 'No, Harry. No, you don't.'

'Don't what?'

She licked her lips. 'You don't get to brush me off.'

There was a flicker at the edge of his eye. 'What do you mean?'

She gestured with one hand and sighed. 'Why? Why do you do that?'

'Do what?'

'Speak to staff like that. Do you even realise that you do it? Micromanaging people. Have you any idea how that makes someone feel? It's almost like you don't trust them to do their job.' She shook her head. 'Not good for staff morale.'

'It's not about staff morale. It's about competent care for the babies that I've operated on.' The words just seemed to snap out of his mouth.

'Why, Harry? We all want these babies to do well. We all want them to survive. We all want to give them the best possible start in life. It's why we do those jobs.' She stepped forward and put a hand on his arm. 'But why do you act the way you do?'

Confusion flooded his face for a few seconds. As if it were taking him a few moments to process her words.

He opened his mouth to speak, and then paused. It was like his shoulders deflated, and some of the air seemed to go out of his body.

He looked at her. He *really* looked at her. And she saw something flicker in his eyes. A decision. It was like he let down a shield—a barrier. The face that he always kept in place for people.

'Something happened just after my very first neonatal cardiac surgery. Something that meant I had to leave for a few days. I'd left strict instructions for the post-op care.' He took a deep breath. 'While I was away. The baby—Joe—became very sick. He threw off a pulmonary embolism. There was nothing anyone could do and by the time I got back he was dead.' Harry twisted his hands together. 'I wished I hadn't gone. It was a family matter. Something no one else could deal with.' He faltered for a second. 'I hadn't even wanted to go in the first place.' He closed his eyes for a second, 'And when I realised what had happened to Joe, I was angry. I was beyond angry. I was sure, if I stayed there in the NICU, I might have picked up on things earlier and been able to stop what happened.'

Esther breathed. It was like little pieces of the puzzle slotting into place in her brain. 'That's why you're so pedantic about instructions?'

He nodded. 'Some people would just call me paranoid. But when you've had one neonatal death that you think you could have prevented, you don't ever want there to be another.'

She pressed her lips together for a moment, reaching across and putting one hand on his. 'But I've been in NICU a long time now, Harry.

You must know that with the best will in the world, and even a sixth sense, we can't predict everything.'

He gave a slow nod. She knew he understood. 'I know that.' His voice broke a little and as she looked up into his eyes she could see how affected by this he'd been. 'But it doesn't mean that I'll ever stop trying.' He closed his other hand over hers. The warmth flooded through her. He'd been nice to her yesterday. He'd reached out. And now she wanted to reach out to him.

'So that's why you deal with staff like that? You're afraid?'

For a moment he said nothing, and then he gave a small, hesitant nod. She kept their hands together. 'You have a good team at the Queen Victoria. You can trust us, Harry. You can trust us with your babies. You might not know that yet, but you have to give us a chance. You have to let us show you that we can do the job you want us to.'

They were so close right now. All she could feel was the heat emanating between their bodies. He'd finally revealed a tiny part of himself, but it felt like just scratching the surface.

She shouldn't ask. She knew she shouldn't. But she couldn't help herself.

'Why did you have to leave, Harry?'

His eyes locked on to hers and her breath caught in her throat, wondering if she'd just pushed him too far.

'My father died,' he said bluntly. 'I had to leave to organise the funeral. There was no one else.' He shook his head, a sheen across his eyes.

'Oh, Harry,' she sighed, and naturally reached up one hand to the side of his face.

He squeezed his eyes closed and his jaw tightened. 'Don't,' he breathed. 'Don't feel sorry for me. We weren't close. We'd never been close. I didn't have a traditional happy family life.' He let out a hollow laugh and stepped back. 'Part of this is all caught up in my anger. I almost blamed my father for dying and ruining the outcome of my first surgery. How bad is that? What kind of a person does that make me?'

Her stomach twisted. There was real hurt in those words. She had no idea what had happened between Harry and his father. The animosity was real, but so was the regret—even if he couldn't see it for himself. Pain practically exuded from his pores.

But now she knew. Now she knew why he acted that way. And she had understood. He had to learn to trust his colleagues, her included.

He looked at her again and she could sense the change in atmosphere from them both. They'd both revealed a tiny part of themselves. Like Harry, she didn't want him to feel sorry for her, but now at least they understood each other's reasons—his, for being pedantic about instructions, and hers, for wanting to work so hard.

If she lit a match in here right now she was sure the place would go up in flames.

She licked her lips. His eyes were watching her every move, and she could feel the tiny little hairs on her body standing to attention underneath the thick robe.

If he just took a few steps forward...

She blinked and breathed in. She was being ridiculous. She knew she was. But the prickles on her skin told her differently. And the way that Harry was looking at her...

'I'd like to take you up on that offer,' she said, her voice coming out much more throatily than she'd expected.

There was a moment of confusion. 'What offer?'

She gave him a slow smile. 'The underwear.'

For a second he didn't move—as if he were processing her words and seeing all the things that lay underneath them. All the sparks she could feel in the air.

He broke their gaze and pulled open the drawer, grabbing a pair of soft jersey boxer shorts and black socks. He held them out to her and as she reached to take them her hand trembled.

His skin brushed against hers. Fingers to fingers.

And before she knew it, his half-full hand closed around her wrist and pulled her towards him.

It wasn't so much a pull. As soon as they'd connected she'd been ready to close the space between them. She didn't wait for him to put his lips on hers. She moved first, going up on tiptoes and letting her hands slide around his neck.

Harry responded easily, his hands anchoring on her hips and his lips locking with hers. This was no slow easy kiss. This was rapid and passionate with a whole host of pent-up frustration.

Her body signalled for her to do more. But she was conscious of the fact she was naked under the robe and Harry was fully dressed. Esther didn't like inequalities. If there was going to be a repeat of this, they would be on even ground.

His hand moved from one hip and tangled in her hair that was still caught in the make-do knot she'd used in the shower. As she kissed him, she inhaled. Catching the clean fresh smell of his shower gel and finding the still-damp hair at the nape of his neck.

Their kiss slowed. Both of them conscious of what could happen next. Esther wasn't ready for that. This was a guy she'd hated a few days ago. Now, she was semi-naked and kissing him in his walk-in wardrobe after he'd revealed a tiny part of himself. Honestly, she couldn't make this up. Her head still didn't quite believe it.

Their lips parted and he rested his forehead against hers for a few seconds. She liked that. A little moment together with both of them catching their breath. There was no embarrassment. No jumping back as if they'd done something wrong. They were two consenting adults. And it had been a long, long time since anyone had kissed her like that. A kiss that left her breathless and panting and listening to the pitter-patter of her heart against her chest.

Harry smiled. 'Well, that was unexpected.'

She gave a small nod. 'Indeed.'

It was a word she didn't use often. But she was feeling kind of speechless.

She stepped back and picked up the underwear and socks that had landed on the floor. 'I better get dressed,' she said quickly.

Harry blinked as if he'd gone somewhere else for a moment. 'Oh, yeah. I have surgery. I'd better get to the hospital.'

As she stepped outside the wardrobe he caught her arm. 'But I'll take you home first.'

She shook her head. 'No way. What time is it anyway? You're usually at the hospital early.

They'll be looking for you. Driving me across town will just hold you up.'

He shrugged. 'That's okay. And I don't think you realise just how early it is. It's just after six. My surgery isn't until 1:00 p.m. I have plenty of time to drop you back home.'

She knew she should say no again. She knew exactly what the traffic would be like across London—even more so when he was battling to get back to the Queen Victoria. But somehow the words wouldn't come out of her mouth.

She loved her job. She didn't mind working hard. But it left so little time for anything else. She *liked* the fact that someone had actually taken the time and trouble to take care of her for once. Her mum was back home in Scotland. Apart from the handful of friends she'd trained with here, she didn't really have any deep friendships. Lots of casual acquaintances from work, but nothing else.

So, even though good manners meant she should probably insist she say no to Harry, the problem was, she just didn't want to.

'Give me five minutes,' she said, turning to leave and trying her best not to look at the giant bed in front of her. She swallowed and shook her head. One kiss. That's all she'd had and she was already starting to have crazy thoughts.

She walked down his corridor, seeing his

wealth everywhere. This guy was a duke, why on earth would he be interested in a midwife from a wee place in Scotland? She wasn't exactly his type. And he wasn't exactly hers.

It was beyond odd that she'd gone in a few days from wanting to plot a guy's murder to thinking about his lips.

She reached her own room, pulled on the clothes and stuffed her own inside her large handbag. There was something intensely personal about slipping her legs into Harry's jersey shorts. They were big for her, and it just made her consider how snugly they fitted him. Esther let out a groan and shook her head. 'Get a grip,' she muttered to herself.

The clothes were miles too big so she cuffed the joggers so they didn't swallow her so much. Then hung the robe back up on the bathroom door. She had a quick check to make sure she hadn't left anything behind, then slipped on her shoes and jacket.

Harry was waiting for her in the middle of the hall and pressed a button revealing a lift.

She blinked and shook her head. 'Your house has a lift?'

He nodded. 'Of course. The car is in the basement downstairs. I think I've used the front door only a handful of times since I moved in.'

She sighed as she stepped in. 'And here was

me thinking you must have carried me up legions of stairs. It's not quite so gallant knowing you just shoved me in a lift and pressed a button.'

He grinned. 'I can assure you, I didn't shove you anywhere. But—' he let out a laugh '—but the lift did help.'

She nudged him. 'If only you'd strained something.'

He turned to her, that gleam back in his eyes again as the door slid open to a dark basement. 'Oh, I think we can definitely agree that I strained something.'

She couldn't wipe the smile off her face as he opened the car door for her and she slid inside, quickly giving him the postcode for her address.

The journey across London was easy, and they chatted all the way. Sometimes about patients, sometimes about other members of staff, and Harry asked a few questions about Esther's mum. There was little point in trying to keep things secret. She'd already told him about her mum's illness and her keeping the family afloat, so nothing seemed intrusive. She kept quiet about her own father. She loved him, she'd adored him, but telling more about him would mean she would have to admit he'd been a dreamer and a drifter. It was why a stable life and stable job were so important now.

But she was curious about him. She wanted to ask more about his relationship with his parents. He'd only said a few sentences. But the resentment he'd had towards his father was very real. She wondered what kind of life he must have had to make him feel like that.

It was a little odd. But she didn't feel as if she could pry. She was acutely aware that one kiss didn't give her the right to ask for a full family history.

They drove into Dagenham and her stomach gave a little flip. She wasn't ashamed of where she stayed, but it was certainly different from his town house in Belgravia. Her basement flat was dark, with cracked windows and a few broken lamp posts nearby. Her whole flat could probably fit into his large bedroom and walk-in wardrobe and she hated the thought he might judge her because of it. Rents were high in London and it was the best she could afford.

As they pulled up outside her flat her phone beeped. She couldn't believe it actually still had any charge left. As she pulled it from her bag it beeped again and she smiled and shook her head. Harry's eyes were still on the road as he manoeuvred to park. 'Something wrong?'

She shook her head. 'Just my friends. Chloe—you might have met her. She works in A&E and covers the air ambulance service too. She's just come on duty and heard I was unwell last night. She's texting to see how I am.'

'She texted twice?'

Esther smiled and shook her head. 'Oh no. The second text is from Carly. She's a community midwife. Chloe will have asked her if she's heard from me, and now Carly is texting too. I bet if I check my emails I'll have one from Isabella too. She trained with us but is in New Zealand right now.'

'They're checking up on you?'

A warm feeling spread across her stomach. She should have known the girls would all contact her as soon as they heard she wasn't well.

Sometimes London felt a bit overwhelming. It didn't matter they all worked in different places. She knew if she picked up the phone to any one of these girls at any point, they would be there for her.

They all understood why she had to work so hard. Chloe frequently told her about extra shifts in A&E.

'They're my friends. We check up on each other.'

Harry gave an approving nod as the car came completely to a halt. She turned her head to the side and caught her breath. She looked at her flat every day. But coming from his plush town house to her basement flat with the row of run-down shops next door didn't make her feel proud.

Before she had a chance to say anything he was out of his seat and holding open the door for her. She climbed out and gave him a smile. Goodbyes could be awkward. 'Trying to get rid of me?' she joked.

'Nope,' he said, his hands going to her hips. 'Just making sure you don't run inside without kissing me goodbye.'

His lips were on hers in an instant. And she didn't resist. She wrapped her hands around his neck again as her body pressed against his. This was brand new, but it felt more comfortable than it should. Although her brain was telling her they lived different lives and had absolutely nothing in common, her body was telling her something different.

Harry wasn't permanent. This could be a passing thing. She could still commit to her work without getting too involved. She might actually have five minutes of fun. It had been so long she'd almost forgotten what it felt like. Hopefully he would be on the same wavelength.

They were in the middle of the street, so after a few moments she pulled reluctantly away, her lips already feeling swollen. 'Rest up and I'll see you at work,' he said.

She watched as he walked back around his

car, slid behind the wheel of the Aston Martin and gave a wave as he drove away.

She wasn't quite sure whether to feel happy or sad. He hadn't asked for her number. He hadn't made any kind of promise or intention.

She took a few deep breaths. Her eyes caught a familiar face walking down the other side of the road. One of the orderlies from the hospital. He gave her the briefest nod and headed on down towards the train station.

Her cheeks flamed. Perfect. So much for keeping things low profile.

As she headed down the steps to her flat, part of her was still frothy and light. It didn't matter how much she wanted to pretend otherwise, Harry Beaumont had definitely gotten under her skin.

CHAPTER SIX

SHE'D SPENT THE day lying on the sofa, eating bite-sized chocolates and drinking tea. It was the first day off she'd had in a month.

By the time she got up the next morning she was feeling much better. It was clear the antibiotics had finally kicked in, and any sign of the previous reaction was completely gone.

There was a definite spring in her step as she walked along the Thames that morning. The NICU was quiet when she entered, which was usually a good sign. It meant things had been fine overnight.

The handover went smoothly and she was pleased to see Billy again. His charts showed he was starting to gain a tiny bit of weight and his wound was clean.

Her phone buzzed in her pocket and she checked. Carly. Take second break. Need to meet you in canteen.

She frowned. Was something wrong? By the

time she reached the canteen, Chloe and Carly were already sitting at a table waiting for her, coffee steaming from mugs and a plate of scones in front of them. As a community midwife Carly didn't spend quite so much time in the hospital so Esther was immediately suspicious.

She pulled her chair out warily, looking from one face to the other. 'What's going on? Does one of you have something to tell me?'

Chloe tilted her head just a fraction to the side. 'Why, that's just what we were about to ask you.'

'Okay, so what does that mean?' asked Esther as she pulled one of the coffee cups towards her.

Carly had mischief written all over her face. 'Should we curtsey?'

Esther leaned her head on one hand. 'You got me. I have no idea what you're talking about.'

Chloe pulled a face. 'Don't forget where I work.'

'I know exactly where you work.' Recognition started to dawn. 'Oh, is this about me being not well?'

Carly drummed her fingers on the table. She obviously wanted to get to the point. 'More about who looked after you when you weren't well.' Cutting right to the chase.

Chloe sliced open one of the scones. 'Viktor came in this morning and took great delight in telling everyone you were in a lip lock with Harry Beaumont early yesterday morning and it was clear he was dropping you off.'

Esther's mouth fell open. She put her head on the table. 'Oh no.' Viktor. The orderly. Of course.

'Oh yes,' said Carly with glee in her voice. 'Now spill, girl. I want to know all the details.'

Esther stayed quiet for a few moments. These were her friends. At least they'd warned her she was the latest piece of hospital gossip.

She pulled her head back up. 'I'm the talk of the steamie, aren't I?'

'Yep,' said Chloe, nodding her head. 'But I want facts, not fiction.' She grinned as she looked at Esther. 'So did you, or did you not, spend the night with Harry Beaumont—our resident duke?'

There it was again—the rush of heat to her cheeks when she thought about Harry. It was getting to be normal for her.

She bit her bottom lip and tried to think of how to put this. These guys were her friends, they weren't going to judge her.

'I was working in A&E and had a bit of re-action to the antibiotics I was on. I'd been feeling tired for days and finally worked out it was due to an infection. The first set didn't work, the second set gave me hives and Harry got me some steroids and checked me over.'

Chloe's eyebrows shot up. 'Checked you over, did he?' Her voice was like a cartoon character.

Esther gave her a nudge. 'Stop it. Because I'd had a reaction they said I could only be discharged if I had supervision. Harry offered to be the supervision. I think he just felt sorry for me, because we'd had a fight a few days before. He took me home that night and I fell asleep in the car. When I woke I was in his town house.'

'Where's his town house?' asked Carly quickly.

'Belgravia.'

Both of her friends gave a little sigh. 'Well, he is a duke,' said Chloe.

'So, you slept all night, *alone*?' asked Carly.

'Yes.' Esther nodded determinedly. 'Alone.'

'So what about the love fest outside your flat, then?' Chloe was smothering her scone with jam.

Esther reached up and grabbed a strand of her hair from her ponytail and started twirling it around her finger. 'Yeah, that.'

'Yeah, *that*,' repeated Carly. 'Get to the real story, we're on a time limit here.'

Esther started stalling, wondering how she could tell the story without a whole heap of mixed emotions swirling around in her head. She buttered her scone ever so slowly.

Chloe let out a big sigh. 'Any time this year, Esther.'

For some reason she couldn't quite meet any of their inquisitive gazes. It was so much easier to stare at the scone, even though her appetite wasn't quite what it should be. Normally the Queen Victoria scones lasted around thirty seconds on her plate.

'Well...' she started slowly. 'He made me breakfast that morning.'

'In bed?' asked Carly.

Esther shook her head. 'No, not in bed, in the kitchen. I'd had a shower and asked him for some spare clothes to change into. He took me into his walk-in wardrobe and while we were in there...'

'While you were in there, what?' Carly pressed.

Chloe laughed and waved her hand. 'Sorry, I stopped paying attention once you said the words "walk-in wardrobe."'

Esther sighed. 'While he passed me some clothes, our hands touched and, well, it was just like...something.'

'Something?' Both girls spoke in unison and leaned forward.

She couldn't tell them the rest. She couldn't

tell them what he'd revealed. It was private. Just like her story about her mum.

'Yeah, something. You know how it is when you meet someone and then all of a sudden there's just this feeling and…then he kissed me.'

'And?' asked Carly.

'And I might have kissed him back,' she admitted.

'Wait a minute,' said Chloe. 'So this guy, who three days ago you texted me and said he was an arrogant git and you hated him, now he's kissing you and you're kissing him back?'

When she said it like that it seemed ridiculous, and Esther cringed. 'Yeah, maybe.'

'And then he dropped you back home and kissed you all over again outside your flat?' said Carly.

Esther nodded. She took a bite of her scone in the hope they might stop asking her questions.

Chloe was grinning, giving Carly a conspiratorial nod across the table. 'Sounds like quite a turnaround.'

'It does.' Carly grinned too and folded her arms across her chest. 'So, like I said, should we start curtseying around you?'

'Oh, stop it, you two.' Esther shook her head and gave a wistful sigh. 'I have no idea what happens next, if anything. He's just passing through. We didn't make plans. He didn't ask for my number. He just said he'd see me at work.' Her stomach gave a squeeze. Saying those words out loud made her feel as if she'd been entirely led on.

For the first time there was silence at the table.

Eventually Chloe spoke up, her voice artificially bright. 'Well, that doesn't mean anything. Maybe he's waiting to see how you react. Maybe he doesn't want to come on too strong.'

'Yeah, that's it,' agreed Carly quickly. 'He's waiting for your lead.'

'Or he's clearly not that interested,' said Esther flatly.

The people at the table next to them stood up and Esther checked her watch. 'Gotta go, time's up.'

Chloe gave her arm a little squeeze. 'This could be a good thing. You might get to have a little fun.'

Esther picked up her bag and gave her a weak smile. 'Let's just wait and see.' It made her feel a bit stupid. Half the hospital would now know she'd locked lips with Harry Beaumont, as gossip spread quicker in the hospital than an infectious disease.

She gave the girls a wave and hurried up the stairs. For the next few days she'd keep her head down. She could only hope that the gossip about her and Harry would pass quickly and move on to someone else.

CHAPTER SEVEN

HARRY NOTICED THE strange atmosphere as soon as he walked in the NICU. Billy was progressing well, and baby Jude had been operated on successfully two days before. He'd had half a mind to ask the sister this morning to allocate both babies to Esther. Working with one midwife was easier than working with two, but that might have seemed a bit presumptuous. Oona didn't strike him as a woman who liked someone else to try and influence her staffing.

There seemed to be lots of strange sideways glances, and he moved over to where Francesca was reviewing a new baby for surgery tomorrow. 'What's going on?' he whispered.

She let out a low laugh. 'Haven't you heard? You and a—' she glanced across the unit to where Esther was standing '—certain midwife are current persons of interest. I hear you got a little friendly with our feisty midwife.'

Harry let out a groan. 'Oh no, where did that

come from?' He hated being gossiped about at work and had learned over the years never to do anything that put him in that position. It seemed he hadn't paid attention to his own advice. That tiny flicker of fire that had flashed through his brain on the drive to work about having a little fun was quickly dying down to an ember.

'Someone down in A&E told me,' Francesca said. 'So I take it that it's true, then?'

He kept his gaze elsewhere. 'Might be,' he said noncommittally. The grin on Francesca's face got wider. She touched his arm. 'Connections, Harry. That's good.'

He felt himself bristle as he moved over towards Esther to check on Billy.

He started to talk to her but she raised her hand. 'Give me a minute.'

He was startled by her apparent brush-off and stood next to Billy's crib as she walked swiftly away. She knocked on a door just away from him. 'Jill, are you okay in there?'

When there was no answer she tried again. Heads started to turn in the unit. Esther's voice wasn't low.

She pulled a coin from her pocket and used it to turn the lock from the outside—a common trick in a hospital. She stuck her head around the door, then pulled it back out. 'Put out an emergency call,' she yelled as she squeezed through the gap in the door.

All the staff moved in unison, Harry included.

He ran straight over, grabbing an emergency trolley behind him. He stuck his head through the gap to see Esther already on the floor, pulling Jill towards her. Jill was collapsed just behind the door, blood pooling on the floor. Esther looked up at Harry. 'I need a trolley.'

'Possible PPH,' he shouted to the staff. 'Can someone find us a trolley?'

Once Esther had pulled Jill over, he slid behind the door after grabbing a few things from the trolley. That was the funny thing about hospital bathrooms—they always seemed a reasonable size until there was an emergency in one of them.

'Does she have a pulse?' he asked.

It didn't matter that Harry's speciality was tiny babies. All tiny babies had a mother and he'd dealt with more than his fair share of obstetric emergencies.

A loud buzzer sounded. The emergency call had gone out.

Esther looked up at him, her face pale. 'Barely,' she said, lowering her head to watch for the rise and fall of Jill's chest. It was clear she was well versed in the protocols. Her fingers remained at Jill's neck.

He ignored the blood on the floor. The volume was great, and he could see a large amount of clots. Jill had clearly come to use the bathroom when she'd collapsed.

'How did you know?' he asked Esther.

'My gut,' she replied. 'I thought she looked off when she said she was going to the bathroom.'

In the few seconds it had taken her to say those words Harry had already inserted a cannula into one of Jill's veins. When someone had lost so much blood it was important to try and replace body fluids as soon as possible.

They didn't need to talk. Esther had already started running the gelofusine through the giving set.

Francesca appeared at the door, took one glance and handed in the bag and mask, which Harry started using. Jill was still breathing, but not nearly enough.

A few seconds later Esther shouted, 'Connected,' as she stood with the IV set, letting it drip through Jill's vein rapidly.

One of the other midwives managed to get part way through the door and connect a BP cuff and monitor to try and get some reading from Jill. Two seconds later, Francesca was back, throwing some gloves towards Esther and Harry.

Harry snapped them on, knowing his trousers were already covered, as were Esther's scrubs.

It was impossible to miss the blood while they were kneeling on the floor.

'Trolley,' came another shout.

Robin, one of the hospital porters, slid through the gap in the door. The space in the toilet seemed smaller by the second. Someone had thought ahead. Robin was covered in a temporary theatre gown and a pair of gloves. He was slight, which was the reason he got through the gap, but before Harry could position himself differently to help, Robin bent down and picked Jill up in his arms. He stood back against the wall, allowing Esther to pull the door inwards and put it against the wall, letting him place Jill on the waiting trolley. At least seven other staff were poised outside, ready to spring into action. One of the midwives grabbed the IV bag from Esther's hands and Francesca took over with the bag and mask, standing on the end of the trolley so she moved with it when it was dashed away.

Harry blinked and looked down. The thing about blood was, even a little could look like a lot when spilled on the floor. Oona appeared in front of them both. 'I'll call Housekeeping. Go clean up, you two. In fact—' she looked Harry up and down '—stay there a sec. I'll bring you both clean scrubs to change into, then hit the showers and change again. You can't walk down the corridors looking like that.'

A few moments later Oona handed the scrubs in, along with a plastic laundry bag. Her mouth gave an almost smile. 'I'm sure you'll both cope with changing in front of each other.'

She knew. Rumours always spread fast in a hospital. Her voice carried as she started to walk away. 'And, Esther, I'll cover your patients. I know you'll want to go and check on Jill.'

They stared at each other in stunned silence for a few seconds after the shocking event. Then Esther's eyes started to fill. 'Oh no...' she said.

He moved over and wrapped his arms around her. Every part of her body was trembling. His was too. He couldn't pretend that what happened hadn't shocked him. Of course it had.

Emergencies always occurred. But that didn't mean that they didn't impact on the staff.

Jill would be in better hands than his. He wasn't an obstetrician. He was a neonatal surgeon. He wouldn't be surprised if Jill was headed directly to Theatre.

Harry stayed exactly where he was. Oona appeared at the door with one of the housekeepers following behind her with a trolley laden with equipment, but Harry just shook his head wordlessly at her, and Oona gave a nod and retreated.

It was five minutes before Esther stopped crying, her breathing steadying. They were still chest to chest and her breathing fell into unison with his. She stepped back and wiped her face. 'Sorry,' she whispered. 'I can't bear the thought of something happening to Jill.' She pointed to the door. 'You've seen out there. She's got no one. Billy's got no one apart from her.' The last few words broke her. Her hands still trembled. 'Why didn't anyone notice anything? Why didn't *I* notice anything?'

He put his hand on her arm. 'Jill might just have been a mother who had no symptoms, or maybe she had symptoms but didn't want to tell us in case we told her she'd have to leave Billy's side.'

There was a flicker of recognition in Esther's eyes. It was clear she knew that was likely to be the truth.

She stared down at the bottom half of her scrubs, moving over to where the clean sets were sitting. She didn't even look at him as she pulled her top over her head, replacing it with a clean one, then peeling the scrubs trousers from her legs. She ran some paper towels under the tap and wiped her legs before pulling on the clean set. Harry mirrored her moves, replacing his shirt and trousers with scrubs, and shaking his head at his shoes before dumping them in a plastic bag. They'd have to go in the disposal. He had spare shoes in his locker.

They stepped outside the bathroom. The

NICU was silent, only the noise of a few monitors in the background. The housekeeper was standing to the side and disappeared silently into the messy bathroom behind them. Esther's feet led her straight to Billy's crib. She placed one hand on the plastic and leaned over, looking down on him. 'Oh, honey,' she whispered. 'I'm going to go and find your mummy. I'll make sure she's okay.'

It was the look on her face that did it for him. He didn't care that every set of eyes on the unit were currently on him. He would never leave a colleague who was upset like this at work.

Often in health care they recognised trauma for their staff and offered counselling or debrief sessions at a later date. But that would be for later, not for now.

He put his arm around her shoulders and guided her away. 'Let's get cleaned up properly. I'll meet you outside the changing rooms once we've showered and changed and we'll check on Jill.'

Esther didn't speak on their long walk down the corridor and he noticed a few heads turn in their direction. He didn't move his arm from her shoulders. He didn't really care what people had to say. It was nobody's business but theirs.

She turned to face him at the changing room door, her blue eyes meeting his. 'Thank you,' she said in a croaky voice, before lowering her head again.

'No, thank *you*,' he said, putting his fingers under her chin and tilting her head towards his. 'You just knew. And you acted. Thank goodness. Jill could have been in the bathroom for much longer. She could have bled out completely. You acting on instinct made all the difference.'

He pressed his forehead down against hers. 'Have faith, Esther. We got her in time.'

As they stood together her hands reached over and squeezed his. It was unexpected. Every move had been his. But this felt just right.

After a moment he reluctantly stepped back. 'Meet you in ten,' he said.

'Meet you in ten,' she repeated as she backed in through the changing room door.

Everything felt like her fault. Her head had been in the clouds, full of daisies and unicorns, when her mind should have been firmly on the job.

Jill's postnatal checks had been routinely carried out every afternoon since Billy's admission, and she hadn't complained of pain or discomfort that morning, so Esther had no reason to change the routine. Her bleeding had been within the normal range, and she'd displayed no obvious temperature. Her notes all said that her uterus was contracting as expected. But none of these things mattered to Esther. What mattered was that Jill had taken unwell while she'd been on shift. She wasn't quite sure what it was that had triggered her bad feeling.

Had Jill pulled a face just as she'd closed the bathroom door? It had to have been something. Something that told her to go and check. And thank goodness that instinct had been there.

Stories of nurse, midwife and health visitor instinct were often described as old wives' tales— similar to a mother's instinct. But Esther didn't believe that for a second. She'd witnessed too many incidents. Too many times there had been no explanation for a health care professional, or a mother, to check in on a patient or child only for them to discover something amiss, for there not to be some kind of explanation for it. One day she'd love to do a scientific study on it. But today was not that day.

She scrubbed her skin in the staff showers, watching the water turn from pale pink to clear. She rarely used these, preferring to shower at home. The hospital towels were always rough and slightly scratchy, so she dried quickly and redressed in yet another set of scrubs.

Harry had been so good to her. So nice. So supportive. It didn't help that everyone had already been looking at them. It didn't matter what the truth was; it was clear that others were assuming that more had happened between Esther and Harry than was true. She wasn't quite sure whether to feel happy or sad about that.

Taking things fast in a relationship had never been Esther's style.

She wasn't even sure that Harry wanted any kind of relationship. She couldn't even sort out her own feelings about it. They were from such opposite ends of the social spectrum. So much about him made her secretly a little mad. Money made life easy for people. And the ease of money just seemed to emanate from him. The voice, his stance, his clothes, even his attitude.

Esther was proud of herself, and her upbringing. Did she really want to associate with someone who, through no fault of his own, could make her feel less of a person? She didn't need that. She didn't want that.

But as she opened the door to the changing room she found Harry leaning on the wall opposite, answering a text on his phone. His white coat was back in place, along with new shoes and clean scrubs. Her heart gave a strange little flip. Making its feeling clear.

'She's in Theatre Five,' Harry said quickly. 'Come on.'

They waited nearly an hour before Jill's obstetrician came out, her face serious. She stuck out her hand straight away. 'Thank you, guys. My girl is only here because you both acted so quickly.'

Esther made a strange little sound at the back of her throat she was so relieved. She knew Dr Gillespie, the obstetrician, well but hadn't been able to read her face at all as she'd walked towards them.

'What happened?' she asked.

Dr Gillespie pulled her theatre hat from her head. 'Part of her placenta was retained. I've no idea why she hadn't reported symptoms. Once we got her into Theatre I thought I was going to have to do a hysterectomy.'

'Did you?' asked Esther.

Dr Gillespie shook her head. 'No, thank goodness. But I suspect she'll need careful observation in any future pregnancies.'

Even though the news was still serious, Esther couldn't help but smile. Jill was alive. She was safe. Billy still had a mum.

Dr Gillespie gave them both another nod, then headed back down the theatre corridor.

'I need to go and tell the staff in NICU,' said Esther.

Harry nodded. 'Of course. Go ahead.'

A smile broke across her face. She stood up on tiptoes and kissed Harry on the cheek.

'Thank you.' She smiled. There was a little cough from someone who walked past.

Harry smiled too. 'Let's give them something to talk about,' he said as he pulled her towards him.

CHAPTER EIGHT

ESTHER STARED AT the smooth envelope pushed through her door. She'd been talking to her mum on the phone and making some toast when she'd noticed the unusual post.

Even running her fingers over it made a little shiver run down her spine. This was expensive stationery.

It must be a mistake, but as she turned it over it was definitely her name that was on the front.

But there was no address. Just her name, in fine script. *Ms Esther McDonald.*

She couldn't help but be intrigued. She slid the envelope open. Inside was a stiff card invitation. She pulled it out and stared at it.

Lord and Lady Brackenridge invite the Duke of Montrose and guest to the Avistock Charity Ball at Eglinton Hall.

There was a cute dinosaur sticky note stuck to the invitation in writing she recognised from the NICU as Harry's. *Will you come with me?*

They hold this event for a kids' charity every year and I don't want to let them down by being a no-show. Harry x.

Esther staggered back onto the sofa, laughter bursting out of her. A ball? Her? Was Harry crazy?

She turned the invite over in her hands. He'd obviously driven to her house and posted it through the door last night. Why hadn't he knocked? Why hadn't he mentioned it at the hospital?

She wasn't quite sure where they were. Harry would be moving on soon. It seemed like the whole hospital were now assuming they were dating and sleeping together. Neither of which were true. She'd never dated anyone she'd worked with before. This was all new territory for her and she wasn't quite sure how to navigate it.

She ran her fingers over the thick card. A ball. Since when did a girl from one of the worst areas of deprivation in Scotland get invited to attend a ball with a duke?

The smile across her face felt infectious. She didn't care how ridiculous it was. She didn't actually care if it just brought home to her how different she and Harry were. For one day it might feel nice to live the life of someone else. To walk in a different set of shoes. Yes, she could worry about a dress, because she knew straight away that there was nothing suitable in her wardrobe, and she certainly couldn't spare the funds to buy something appropriate. But that's what friends were for. Before she even gave herself time to think about it she shot off a text to Carly and Chloe.

OK, girls, I've been invited to a ball. You've seen my wardrobe. The Princess Leia costume and gold hot pants are not going to cut it. Anyone got something I can wear?

Instantly she could see little dots appear on her phone.

Chloe sent a row of laughing emojis followed by a line of question marks.

Carly's reply made her heart jump. I've got just the thing. Dark navy ball gown with a little bit of sparkle. Will leave it in NICU for you later today.

Esther tried not to let out a squeal. They were roughly the same size so she knew it would fit fine.

Perfect. Now she knew she had something to wear she just had to worry about everything else. Like how it would feel to be Cinderella at the ball…

* * *

Harry wasn't quite sure he was playing this right. And those thoughts were strange to him, because he'd never really been in a relationship where he'd worried about things like that.

The issue was, the whole hospital assumed that he and Esther were a 'thing.' And to be honest, that didn't bother him at all. Because he was only passing through.

Sure, he'd heard all the things about not mixing business with pleasure. But over the years he'd known lots of colleagues who'd had relationships with workmates. Some good, some bad.

As soon as he'd received that invitation he'd thought immediately about Esther. He'd driven over to her house, stuck a little note on it and put it through her door. She'd smiled at him the next day in NICU and said she'd be glad to come.

And that had been the point he'd realised he hadn't *really* been thinking about Esther. He hadn't thought that going to a charity ball with him might mean turning down an extra shift she could do, or that she would have to conjure up something suitable to wear. Part of him had wanted to go back and offer to buy her something. But somehow he knew Esther would find that completely insulting.

So, here he was, sitting outside her door,

waiting to pick her up. He pulled at the sleeves of his jacket as he stepped outside the car and walked down the dark steps to her front door. She opened it on the first knock, a broad smile across her face.

A scent of orange blossom floated towards him and he wasn't quite sure if it was coming from her, or the flat.

The room behind her was compact but immaculate. There was a large squishy red sofa, with a coffee table in front, perched on a colourful rug. The floor was the laminate that lots of people had now, and in the back of the room he could see a neat white kitchen.

Photos were everywhere. Adorning her mantelpiece, walls and tables. All of family, and even from here he could see that most of the photos had people with their arms wrapped around each other, laughing.

Something twisted deep inside. He couldn't ever recall a moment in his life where he'd been at an event with his parents that resembled anything like this. The moment, the warmth, the adoration.

Never. His life had never replicated anything like that. For a split second all he could feel was envy. Envy for her simpler, and yet immensely fuller, life. He pushed those thoughts away.

His eyes went automatically back to Esther. 'Wow,' was the only word he could form.

She was wearing a long navy gown. The shoulders and cap sleeves of the dress were part-sheer, with sequins scattered across the top, then the middle was ruched, emphasizing her waist, then the sheer navy fabric fell in layers to the floor, making a light swishing sound whenever she moved. Her dark hair was piled on top of her head with a few tendrils escaping at the sides, accentuating her sparkling blue eyes, which were fixed directly on him. The effect was dazzling.

Esther beamed. Literally beamed—it was like a glow was coming off her. One that she clearly didn't see herself.

'Wow yourself,' she said lightly. 'It's not every day I see you in a tux.'

He paused for a few seconds, taking in the full view of her.

Hospitals were odd places. He saw the same faces in virtually the same clothes. There were so many other things going on there that it frequently didn't give anyone time to stop and really look at the people around them.

Now he could see it all. The shine of her hair, the bounce, even though it was tied up in some elaborate way on her head. The swoosh of her long skirts. The cinch of the fabric on her curves. He was looking at her with new eyes, just like the way she was looking at him.

He tugged at his collar, instantly self-conscious. 'I definitely don't wear this every day. But today is a special occasion.'

'Yeah, it is,' she whispered. His mouth was dry. For a second he wanted the world to stop. He wanted to stay and look at Esther the way she was looking at him. He wanted to forget about the ball. And forget about anything else. He wanted to close the door behind them and kiss her right now.

There was something about being in her company. Tonight was about tradition. About being a duke. Nothing in his life to do with his title had ever felt like fun. But tonight, going to the ball with Esther, was the first time he'd actually really, really looked forward to doing something. After a shaky start, she was beginning to become that person for him. The one he actually enjoyed spending time with. This part of his life—the duke stuff—had always been separate. His stomach coiled for him in an unusual way. She didn't even know it, but she was opening up other doors in his mind. Places that had been closed for so long.

Esther blinked. Breaking the spell he was casting in his head.

She gave a thoughtful nod as he gestured to the stairs. "Ready to go? Your carriage awaits.'

They were in the car a few minutes later, crossing London towards Eglinton Hall.

'Tell me about Lord and Lady Brackenridge,' she said as she settled into the seat, 'and tell me more about this charity ball.'

Harry gave a nod. It was only fair that he gave her some background to the event they were about to attend. It was one of the few things he'd continued to go to since the death of his father.

'I've known them since I was a child. Their two daughters are just a few years younger than me. They had a son—Gavin—who died from neuroblastoma when we were all teenagers. It's still rare, but even less was known about it then. They had their first charity ball a few years after Gavin died. They choose a different children's charity to support every year, and I've always gone along.' He paused, taking a breath for a moment. 'Originally the invite was for my parents, but for the last ten years it's come to me.'

'You don't have any siblings?'

Harry shook his head. 'Nope. Just me. I think I was enough of an inconvenience to them.'

Esther's head spun around in surprise. 'What do you mean by that?'

He bristled, not quite sure how to answer the

question. But it was his own fault. He shouldn't have made that comment.

But it was too late. There was no point lying about it. 'I don't think they were really the parenting type.'

He could tell that Esther found that statement surprising. 'Why's that?' she asked.

He gave a shrug. 'It was probably more of a duty thing.'

There was a few moments' silence. 'Okay, I have to admit, I don't get it. What do you mean?'

He snaked his way through the traffic, his hands gripping the steering wheel probably a lot harder than he needed to. 'Duty,' he sighed. 'The duke title is inherited—passed down to the male heir. I'm quite sure they had me to ensure the title passed on.'

From the corner of his eye he could see Esther wrinkling her nose. 'But what if they'd had a girl?'

He let out a low laugh. 'She probably would have been treated as if she was worthless and they would have kept trying for a boy. Thankfully for everyone, that didn't happen. My mother only had to go through a pregnancy once, and when I was born she made it very clear to everyone she had no intention of ever doing it again.'

'Wow,' said Esther softly. 'It sounds kind of medieval.'

Harry nodded. 'Yeah, that's about the size of it. Children should be seen and not heard was very much the mantra in my family. I had a nanny until I was five. Then I spent the rest of my time at boarding school—often during the holidays too—and then at university.'

Esther's head shook. 'I just can't imagine a life like that.' Then her hand shot up to her mouth as she realised how that might sound. 'Oh no, I—'

He stopped her by putting his hand on her leg. 'It's fine, Esther. It is what it is. I had a roof over my head, food in my stomach at all times. I know plenty of kids who had a far worse upbringing than me. These people tonight, Lord and Lady Brackenridge? They were probably the only adults I met who showed any warmth towards me.' He pulled a face. 'Of course, I didn't realise at the time they were trying to match me to one of their daughters.'

Esther let out a gasp. 'This is like a blooming TV show.'

He shot her a glance. 'Yeah, but am I the hero, or the villain?'

Her hand threaded over the top of his, which was still on her leg. 'Oh, I think we can safely say you're the hero.' Her eyes glinted. 'But I'll let you know if you slip.'

He couldn't help but laugh. 'Don't worry. These people are actually fine. They realised pretty quickly that I wasn't a good match for either Penelope or Priscilla.'

'Penelope and Priscilla? That's really their names?' He could hear the disbelief in her voice.

'Oh yes. That's their names. They used to be part of a larger group of friends but I haven't seen either of them in a while. Priscilla is a barrister and last I heard she was dating some millionaire businessman. Penelope has had three engagements—maybe four—each ring bigger than the last. I think she's dating some actor now.'

Esther looked a little stunned. 'Hmm, how the other half lives,' she said quietly.

All of a sudden he realised she might be a bit intimidated by all this. He squeezed her thigh. 'Don't worry,' he said. 'Tonight should be fun.' He wasn't sure if he was trying to reassure her, or himself.

'Hmm…' Esther fixed her eyes on the view outside. He could tell she was thinking. Had he read all this wrong?

He'd wanted to take her out. He'd wanted to take her somewhere special. Of course he did.

And this invitation had given him the perfect excuse. Didn't people like balls?

The girl he'd first met as a crabby midwife was sitting next to him looking like perfection, but he could see her knotting her hands in her lap. He hadn't meant to make her uncomfortable. Or maybe it wasn't the ball. Maybe it was the fact he'd just revealed a bit more about himself and his difficult relationship with his parents. He knew that she adored her mother, and maybe she hadn't liked the fact he'd been so up front about how things had been totally different in his household.

He'd tried his best to forget about that part of his life. His heritage was always there. The title a daily reminder. But Harry actively chose not to use it on a regular basis. He introduced himself to everyone as Harry Beaumont, neonatal surgeon. Not as Harry Beaumont, Duke of Montrose.

As he pulled his car up the long, winding drive of Eglinton Hall, he'd already made up his mind. They'd only stay as long as they had to. If he had to, he could use a patient as an excuse for leaving. But the truth was, Billy, his mother and baby Jude were all doing well. He had four more surgeries scheduled in the next few days, with two babies being transferred from other hospitals, and two mothers whose babies had cardiac issues delivering in the Queen Victoria especially so their babies could go straight for surgery with Harry.

This was practically his only night off for a while, so he intended to use it well.

'Busy place,' murmured Esther as they joined the line of cars filing up to the main doors with liveried staff opening the doors, then whisking the cars away again.

Harry gave her a worried smile as they pulled up next. Waiting as she walked around the car and holding out his arm for her as they climbed the steps.

This night would be good. He'd make sure of it.

Cinderella had arrived in a horse-drawn carriage, and Esther arrived in an Aston Martin. She wasn't sure which one was better.

Carly's dress was a dream. She gathered the skirts in her hand as they climbed the stairs and stepped into the biggest reception hall she'd ever seen.

This whole place was magnificent. From the impressive sand-coloured stone building, the elegant windows and the four towers at each corner of the house. Except it wasn't a house. Not in the normal sense. It was one of those gorgeous mansions owned by the rich, the very rich and the very, very rich. The size and scale reminded her of Kelvingrove Museum in Glasgow that she'd visited as a school kid when it housed Egyptian relics and dinosaur bones.

Who actually lived in a place like this?

The huge reception hall had tiny white and black tiles on the floor that looked like marble. The walls were covered in dark wood panels but the whole place felt light and airy, brightly illuminated by the biggest chandelier she'd ever seen.

Staff stood with silver trays of long-stemmed glasses at the entrance way to a room on the right. Harry nodded at a few people casually. He wasn't stunned by these surroundings at all. He seemed quite at home as he led her through to the next room. Voices were low as people chatted and sipped their champagne.

Thank goodness for Carly. Although Esther was quite sure the dress she was wearing had probably cost a lot less than most of the other female guests' gowns, she didn't feel out of place at all. Most wore full-length gowns. Some beautiful. Some daring. And some just a little...strange.

But Esther's felt fine in comparison. Nearly every gentleman wore a tux like Harry's. She shot him a sideways glance. But every gentleman didn't look half as good as Harry did. She could see him getting admiring glances from other women. But his arm had slid around her waist as they'd entered this room, and there it firmly remained. It made her heart flutter in a way she wasn't ready to acknowledge.

'Harry!' came a deep voice near to them. A tall man came over, arm outstretched, and shook Harry's hand enthusiastically, gripping his arm with his own hand. 'I'm so glad you're here.' He leaned over conspiratorially. 'You can always help me hide when it gets too much.'

Harry's smile was broad and genuine. 'Lord Breckenridge—David—I'd like you to meet my good friend Esther McDonald.'

The older man turned towards her, shaking her hand just as enthusiastically as he'd shook Harry's. 'It's a real pleasure—any friend of Harry's is always welcome.' He turned and waved over to a woman behind them. 'Sabrina, Harry's here.'

The woman was dressed in black satin, her grey hair pinned elegantly back. She didn't walk; instead, she seemed to glide over to meet them, encompassing Harry in a hug. He kissed both of the woman's cheeks. 'So nice to see you.'

After his comments in the car she'd wondered what to expect. But his affection for this pair was obvious, and Esther was secretly relieved. What must it have been like to grow up with parents who treated you as if you were merely part of the furniture?

The woman wasn't only elegant, she had an old-world charm about her. She spoke to Esther, asking her questions about her job, and seemed genuinely interested in her answers.

For the first time, the initial fear of fitting in, in a place like this, finally started to leave Esther.

'It's so nice to see Harry bring a friend,' Lady Brackenridge said in her ear.

'Thank you for having me.' Esther smiled. 'Harry told me you have the ball every year in memory of your son. I was so sorry to hear about him.'

Lady Brackenridge put her hand on Esther's arm and gave it a little squeeze. 'It was a long time ago. But I still miss him every day. Just like I should.' She put her hand up to her heart. 'Harry and Gavin were such good friends. I've always looked out for him.'

There was genuine affection in her eyes and Esther spoke carefully. 'He seems so comfortable around you both—and comfortable here too. That's nice. He told me about his difficult relationship with his father.'

'He did?' Lady Breckenridge's eyes went wide. She glanced at Harry and her head gave a little nod. Her lips gave a hint of a smile and she shot Esther an approving look. 'I'm glad. Harry is nothing like his father—or his mother for that matter. I always hoped that Harry and his father would make up before the duke died. But it wasn't to be. Old age didn't suit the duke. It just made him more ill-tempered and irrational than before, and poor Harry always bore the brunt of it.' She leaned towards Esther and cupped her cheek. 'You, my girl, might just be the joy that Harry has always been looking for.'

Esther jerked a little at the unexpected affectionate movement. It made her stomach flutter, partly with warmth, and partly with the fear of the expectation that seemed to have just descended on her. Lady Brackenridge spun around as someone came up behind her, greeting her loudly.

There was a loud announcement at a door just ahead. 'Guests, you are kindly invited to take your seats for the Avistock Charity Ball.'

Harry appeared out of thin air and held out his elbow for Esther again. She was still digesting what Lady Brackenridge had said, a tiny swell of panic in her chest. This was temporary. This was just supposed to be fun. She slipped her arm through his and followed the crowds through the double doors.

The ballroom was opulent, decorated in gold and white. Large round tables, covered in white linen with twenty seats at each, covered the expanse of the room. Harry gave their names and they were given a table number. As they sat down, Esther picked up the little card in front of them.

It was a programme for the auction and her stomach muscles tightened. Of course. A charity auction. Realisation flooded over her as other guests took their seats at the table.

Of course. A charity auction with a programme of items up for bids. A shopping trip at one of London's most exclusive stores. Four seats at an extremely popular football cup final. Four seats and travel to an even more popular European football cup final. A box at a show in New York that had a years-long waiting list for tickets. VIP tickets to a gig by one of the biggest pop stars.

Esther's hand went automatically to her champagne glass, which she instantly downed—her mouth had never felt quite so dry. One of the staff placed some plates of hors d'oeuvres on the table. Esther hid her smile. The food was actually so small it could hardly be seen.

Harry leaned closer, his cheek brushing against hers. 'What are you smiling at?'

She looked up at him. He was so close she could see every eyelash and the pale gold flecks in those toffee eyes. She kept her voice low. 'I'm just thinking that if you served those in a pub in Scotland you'd have your head in your hands to play with.'

He let out a low laugh and shook his head. 'I love your crazy expressions.'

'Oh, I have lots more where those came from.' She blinked.

'And I want to hear them all,' he whispered, moving closer.

'Harry!' The voice came from directly behind them and they jumped apart.

He cleared his throat a little awkwardly. 'Penelope! How nice to see you.'

A woman with blond hair wound over one shoulder and an enviable figure slid into the chair on the other side of Harry. She was wearing a bright cerise pink dress that clung to every curve. She flung her arms around Harry and kissed him on both cheeks—just a little too close to his lips—leaving her bright red lipstick on him like some kind of marker. Esther stiffened in her seat.

A waft of expensive perfume floated across the table towards her. Harry returned the hug, a little less enthusiastically, before sitting back in his chair and allowing Esther an even better view of a woman who could simply be described as perfection.

'Penelope, I want you to meet my good friend

Esther McDonald, who has accompanied me tonight.'

Penelope didn't seem at all perturbed. She slid her arm across Harry's body, showing a set of immaculate pointed nails, exactly the same colour as her dress, inviting Esther to shake her hand. 'Pleasure to meet you, Esther.' She beamed.

Esther gulped and shook the hand far more limply than she intended to. Wicked thoughts immediately dashed through her mind. Like how Penelope could easily whip a man's testicles off with one swipe of her nails. She could see Penelope having a quick glance at Esther's short blunt nails. Just the way a nurse's should be. But Esther couldn't help wishing she had put on a quick coat of nail varnish before she'd left the house tonight.

Penelope slid forward, one arm draping conspiratorially around Harry's neck. 'So, how did you two meet?'

It was the voice. It was delicious. Like syrup. All accented, immaculate sounds. Esther knew her own accent was thick. She liked it that way. A few times she'd purposely spoken much quicker than usual in order to put another person firmly in their place. A Scots accent could do that—particularly when dealing with a drunk in A&E. There was a real no-nonsense attitude about a thick Scottish accent that Esther relished.

But tonight? It just made her feel uncouth.

She tried to speak properly, dulling her accent and finishing every word. 'We met at work,' she said, ignoring the look that Harry shot her. 'I'm a midwife in NICU.'

Penelope blinked. 'What's NICU?'

'Prem babies,' said Esther quickly.

Penelope slapped her other hand on Harry's chest—and left it there. 'Oh, of course. Silly me.'

Her eyes went between them both, her smile getting wider. 'So, you met at work. That's kind of cute.'

Harry shifted in his seat. Esther was suddenly intensely aware that on both times Harry had introduced her—first to Penelope's parents, and then to Penelope—he'd described her as a 'good friend.' What did that mean exactly? It was sort of bland. Sort of nothing. Or at least nothing important.

Was that what they were? They hadn't even had that conversation yet. And Esther didn't like the way that burned inside.

She was also trying really, really hard not to bristle at the way Penelope had draped herself possessively around Harry. The girl wasn't giving off vibes. The kind of 'I was here first' thing you sometimes got with exes. Instead, she was showing how comfortable she was around Harry.

Penelope waved her hand for some more wine and a waiter appeared immediately. He lowered his head to Penelope's. 'My usual,' she said easily. 'Harry's too, and—' she leaned forward '—pick your poison, Esther.'

Esther didn't miss a heartbeat. She named a tonic wine that was commonly known in Scotland. Something she was entirely sure a posh place like this wouldn't have in a million years. She wasn't quite sure why she did it.

Was it because she already knew she didn't fit in and wanted to send a message that she had no intention of conforming? She didn't even like that tonic wine, and hadn't touched it since she was a teenager. But it was like all her spiny prickles were coming out at once.

Penelope blinked and smiled. 'Never heard of that one.' She repeated it to the waiter, who quickly disappeared.

A tuxedo-suited man stepped up to the podium at the end of the room, announcing the start of the auction. Penelope shot Esther an excited glance. 'Which one do you want to bid on?'

Every cell in Esther's body prickled. She was almost sure that Penelope didn't mean to make her uncomfortable. The woman had a generally welcoming nature. Maybe she just believed the rest of this room was just as rich as she was. But Esther had already told her that she and Harry worked together. Did she honestly expect a NHS worker to have funds to spend on the charity auction?

Within a few minutes Esther realised that the bidding here wasn't for the faint-hearted. Her knuckles were turning white holding the programme as the bids climbed and climbed.

The room felt oppressive, as if the heat were closing in around her. The waiter appeared back with the drinks. He shot Esther a grin as he lowered her familiar drink next to her. 'None of the monk's wine,' he said, revealing his Scots accent. She started. Only someone who'd been brought up in Scotland would know that the traditional tonic wine was made by monks. The man's eyes gleamed as he sat down a tall glass in front of her. 'So I brought you our other favourite.'

Esther laughed out loud as she looked at the bright blue liquid topped by ruby red, a memory of home shooting through her. She hadn't even been much of a drinker as a teenager, but this definitely reminded her of stale village halls and sitting in the park on a summer's day.

Harry leaned closer. 'What on earth is that?'

'A bit of my past.' She grinned, taking a sip and grimacing.

'What's in it?' he asked.

'Vodka and port.' She pushed it towards him. 'Try it.'

He took a tentative sip and wrinkled his nose. 'It tastes like...' He paused, clearly trying to place it.

Esther named a popular fruity carbonated drink.

'That's it,' he said, throwing his hands up.

'Harry Beaumont, thank you for your bid.'

Esther felt the colour drain from her as Penelope let out a shriek of laughter. Her hand landed on Harry's arm again. 'Oh, you clown. Do you know what you just bid on?'

He sat back in his chair, looking relaxed, if a little stunned. Esther couldn't breathe. She felt sick. This was her fault.

Penelope opened her programme and pointed to something. 'Here. You've just bid on a two-day break in a cottage in Scotland.'

Harry shrugged. 'How much did I bid?'

'Twenty thousand,' said Penelope, as if she'd just mentioned a sum of money that bought a chocolate bar.

'Oh, okay,' said Harry, barely blinking.

'Okay?' All heads at the table turned to Esther's incredulous voice. Inside she felt like she was dying. Harry had just spent twenty thousand pounds by mistake and he didn't seem the least bit bothered. Just how rich was this guy?

That thought alone made her immensely uncomfortable.

Penelope leaned in front of Harry and gave Esther a comforting grin. 'Don't worry. That's spare change to this guy.'

Esther just couldn't find words. She sat back in her chair and watched the spots form in front of her eyes. She'd never felt more like Cinderella in her life. This must be some kind of warped fairy tale.

The auction continued and she sat in a blur. Every cell in her body told her she should be apologising to Harry for being part of the mistake, but she could see he honestly wasn't the least bit bothered and that worried her much more than a blazing argument over whose fault the errant bid was.

Money meant everything to her. In a horrible, materialistic, never-admit-to kind of way. She counted every single penny. She had to, in order to help her mum. Five days out of seven she would pack her lunch. She only allowed herself a coffee from the cart on the Thames twice a week. She couldn't remember the last time she'd bought herself something new to wear. Why buy more clothes when she had perfectly reasonable ones in her cupboard?

A thought of her own life back in Scotland shot into her head. How different it was. This place was all smoke and mirrors. The words Lady Brackenridge had spoken were stuck in her mind. Harry hadn't experienced the same love that she had. Would she have swapped her parents and small house in Scotland for a life like this? Never.

She kept her face perfectly calm as she took some long slow breaths in and out. Harry's hand had crept over to hers and his fingers intertwined with hers. Tingles shot up her arm. Tingles that she really liked.

But this was wrong. Nothing about her and Harry was a match.

She watched as he chatted easily to Penelope. The girl was gorgeous. She seemed genuinely nice and every now and then tried to include Esther in the conversation. But they were talking about friends and casual acquaintances—people that had never, and would never, move in the same circles as Esther.

The more she watched, the more she felt a distance grow between her and Harry. Penelope was a good match for him. She was beautiful. She was intelligent. She fitted easily into his life.

Not like Esther, with her extra shifts and shabby flat.

Even though she was sitting here in Carly's

beautiful gown, her previous confidence was ebbing away little by little.

Then all of a sudden the auction was over. The guests all stood as the tables were removed and a band was spirited in through another door. The music began as waiters started to circulate with drink-filled trays again.

Harry gestured towards one and Esther shook her head. 'No thanks. Want to keep a clear head for tomorrow.'

'You're working again?'

She nodded. 'Just my normal shift in NICU. I'm looking forward to it. I want to see my babies, and I want to see Jill.'

Harry gave a nod as the music changed. He held out one hand towards her. 'How's your dancing?'

'Rave or highland?' she asked cheekily.

He gave a surprised jerk at the spectrum. 'I was kind of thinking of something slower,' he said. Her hand was now in his and he pulled her closer and slid his hand around her waist.

It didn't matter how much her brain had been screaming at her. Telling her that she and Harry weren't a match in any sense. Her heart wasn't listening at all. It was beating wildly at the feel of his body against hers.

His hand slid up to the bare skin at her neck and brushed some of her fine hairs that escaped from the top of her head. The touch was like butterflies on her skin, their wings flapping in a tickly sort of way.

His face broke into a smile, one that only seemed for her. 'You okay?' he asked.

She wanted to spill out a whole lot of answers. But she remembered him in the car, talking about his parents. The expression on his face. It was the first time she'd seen Harry looking vulnerable and less than confident.

She couldn't offload onto him. It didn't seem right. She licked her lips. 'I guess I'm just seeing how the other half live.'

A frown creased his brow as he moved her smoothly around the floor in time to the music. 'You're not happy? Do you want to leave?'

For a second she saw his eyes scan the room, looking back to the bar where Penelope was sipping wine and talking to someone.

She stiffened. She couldn't help it. Maybe he was embarrassed by her, tired of her, and would prefer to spend time in the company of his peers. 'Do you want me to?'

He stopped dancing and looked down at her. 'No. Why on earth would you think that?'

Esther's heart felt as if it were fluttering against her chest wall. 'I... I just...' The words stuck somewhere in her throat. She was making a mess of this.

His hand came down and slid through her hair, resting at the back of her neck. His mouth only inches from her face. 'Esther, I'm sorry if I've made you uncomfortable. I thought you might like it tonight. Maybe I wasn't thinking… maybe I should have—'

She put her finger up to his lips and shook her head. 'I don't think this is about you, Harry. I think we're just different. Different lives, different backgrounds.'

'Opposites attract.' He looked her straight in the eye.

Part of her heart ached for him when she thought about what Lady Brackenridge had said earlier. But this close up to Harry, she could feel her pulse rate rising.

She couldn't help but smile. 'I might know a guy who told me that.'

He leaned forward and kissed her. 'Then trust him. I think I know that guy too. He's okay— in fact, I think he wants to take you to dinner.'

Every part of her wanted to wrap her hands around his neck and keep kissing him. But they were in the middle of a ballroom with five hundred other people; it was hardly appropriate. She leaned back. 'He does?'

'He absolutely does.' Harry grabbed her hand and led her straight across the dance floor, dodging the other people and not stopping to speak to anyone. He pulled his phone from his pocket and made a one-minute call. His car pulled up moments later and he held the door open for her.

She clicked her seat belt. 'Harry, what are you doing?'

'Taking you to the place I should have done earlier.'

She twisted her head at the rapidly vanishing hall behind them. 'But what about your friends?'

He shook his head, his dark eyes meeting hers, and he halted at the bottom of the driveway. 'I'm not interested in them. I'm interested in you.'

'Oh.' It was the only answer she could find. The traffic was much lighter now and they crossed London easily, pulling up and parking on a street she was unfamiliar with.

He came around and opened her door again, then bent down and lifted the hem of her dress just an inch. 'What are you doing?' She let out a high-pitched kind of squeal.

'Checking your shoes. How do you think they'll do on cobbles—want me to carry you?'

She'd only had a few seconds to consider the question before he swept her up into his arms and started striding down a street just around the corner.

'Hey!' She let out a laugh as he covered the

street easily, stopping outside a red wooden door and setting her down gently.

He knocked on the door and Esther leaned back to see the front of the building. She could see a small sign in French, along with a sign for the famous stars that were awarded to restaurants around the globe.

The door opened and a short man with a broad smile greeted them. 'Don't say I'm not good to you.' He nodded to Harry.

Harry took Esther's hand again and led her up a flight of stairs. The restaurant he led her into was small and welcoming, and completely empty.

She spun around. 'Where is everybody?'

He held out his hands. 'It's ours, for the night.'

The short guy appeared again behind them and held out his hand to Esther. 'Armand.' He nodded his head towards Harry. 'It seems I'm your personal chef for the night.'

Esther's eyes widened. 'What? No way.'

Armand gave a casual shrug. 'What can I say? I owe him. He asks for the restaurant for the night, he gets it.'

Armand waved his hand and started to walk to the kitchen, then paused, his hand on the door. 'Any allergies?'

Esther shook her head.

'Anything you absolutely won't eat?'

She shook her head again.

'Oh good, then let me go and create for you something wonderful. Help yourself to wine, Harry,' he shouted over his shoulder as he disappeared into the kitchen.

Esther shook her head and held out her hands. 'How on earth do you get a starred restaurant for the night?'

Harry held out a chair for her. 'The place officially closed last night for refurbishment. So I knew it would be empty tonight. The work doesn't start until next week.'

'And Armand is a friend of yours?'

He grinned as he selected a bottle of wine. 'Armand actually did his first two years of med school with me. But he had a change of heart. His dream was being a chef, not a doctor, and he followed his heart.'

She watched as he poured the wine into the glasses on the table. This all seemed so surreal. She took a small sip. 'So, how does he owe you?'

Harry made an awkward kind of sound as he sat opposite her. 'I gave him the backing to start his first restaurant.'

'Oh.' She wasn't quite sure how to reply to that one. She had no idea what that amount of money would have been, but she was sure enough to know it wouldn't have been insubstantial.

'He's paid it all back.' Harry gave a smile. 'So he doesn't really owe me. It's just a figure of speech.'

Esther sipped the wine again and tried to ignore the little tight coil currently in her stomach. It had eased a bit since they had left Eglinton Hall.

She rested her head on one hand. 'I can't believe you did this.'

Harry looked surprised. 'Why not? Don't you think you're worth it?'

All she could do was blink, because those words hit a whole bunch of nerves she didn't even realise she had. It was like a chilly breeze over her skin. She didn't lack confidence as a person. She knew she was good at her job. And she was comfortable in her own skin. But tonight, in a place that had practically smelled of money, she been distinctly *uncomfortable*. And Esther didn't like feeling like that. Every cell in her body had practically told her to leave.

But there was more than that. It was something much deeper, much more fundamental. *Being worth it.* Those words mattered so much. When her father had flitted from one job to the next, leaving the financial security to her mother, she'd seen how much his every decision hurt her mother. She'd seen her mother's confidence slowly and surely ebb away. They'd both still loved him. He didn't realise how his actions hurt the women in his life. But him, constantly choosing to move on to another job—none of which had been close to home—had always left Esther with a feeling of not being worth staying for.

She never talked about it. Never discussed it. Because then she would have to admit the rose-tinted memories she kept of her father weren't perfect. That he'd hurt them both. But Harry's words had struck a chord. Much deeper than she'd expected.

'Because I think you are,' Harry added. He'd been watching her for the last few seconds, as if he was giving her space to think.

Her phone beeped and she automatically pulled it from her bag—glad of the temporary distraction. She took a breath as she tried to straighten out her thoughts. 'My mum, just let me reply.'

Something flashed across Harry's face. An expression she hadn't really seen before from him. Was that regret? She tapped the keys on her phone quickly and pressed Send, pushing the phone to her side.

Armand appeared a moment later and set two plates down. The aromas instantly drifted up around her. 'Just as well you gave me that warning call,' he said to Harry. 'Enjoy!' He waved his hand and darted back to the kitchen.

Esther laughed. 'How on earth does he move so quickly?' Her hands had automatically picked up her knife and fork. When something smelt this good she didn't want to wait.

'It's one of his many talents,' said Harry as he picked up his cutlery too. 'Dig in. I'm hoping you'll love it.'

And she did. All eight courses that Armand supplied. The food was delicious, the portion sizes just right. She stuck with the one glass of wine, sipping it slowly between courses.

There was something about having the place to themselves. Both of them seemed to relax more. The anxieties of earlier slipped away.

'Have you settled in at the Queen Victoria?' Esther asked as they finished their puddings.

'I think so. We've agreed protocols between hospitals for transfers.'

'So, you'll be at the Queen Victoria more than before?'

He nodded. 'I'm still just a visiting surgeon. It just gives me a base when I get referrals from other counties.'

'Will you still do surgeries in other countries?'

He sighed. 'Of course. I go where the babies are. Staying in random hotel rooms around the world is what I do best.' He paused for a second. 'But I have to admit the facilities that the Queen Victoria have for parents are far superior than any others I've come across.'

Esther nodded in agreement. They didn't just have the parent beds in NICU. The Queen Victoria also had a series of apartments where whole families could stay if their children required long-term care. She wasn't quite sure why she'd started questioning him so much about his job. Or why some of his answers disappointed her. It was ridiculous. Nothing had changed. He was a visiting surgeon. He would come. He would go. She'd known that right from the start. So why did that make her stomach twist and turn?

'Don't you wish you could be somewhere more permanent? Have your own team? Stay in your house instead of random hotel rooms?'

She watched as his shoulders tensed. The far-off expression on his face made her want to reach out and hug him.

'Home? What does that even mean?' He didn't even try to hide the huskiness in his voice.

Her heart squeezed in her chest. Did Harry really not have a sense of home? How must that feel? How did a child grow up when they never had the sense of warmth and love that she'd experienced?

She clasped her hands in front of her. 'Home is the place you can be yourself. The place you're most comfortable, and the people you're most comfortable with. Where you don't need any masks, or faces. Where you can be exactly who you want to be.'

She was remembering the expression on Lady Brackenridge's face. Remembering some of the things that she'd said—and wondered if she'd said too much.

She almost jumped as Harry stood up, the chair scraping on the floor behind her. He held out his hand towards her.

'Esther, will you come home with me tonight?'

She held her breath. He didn't need to say anything else out loud. He wasn't just asking her back to Belgravia. He wasn't just asking her back to the pristine town house that didn't really look as if anyone lived there.

She knew exactly what he was asking. She licked her lips and swallowed. All the fears and uncertainties she'd had back at Eglinton Hall threatened to swamp her.

She was with Harry. The guy she'd initially hated, but now was slowly but surely stealing little parts of her heart. They'd only kissed up until this point. But she couldn't ignore the attraction that flared in her body every time she glimpsed him. Every time she caught a waft of his aftershave. Every time his skin came into contact with hers.

For the last few hours she'd let herself be swamped by all the differences in wealth between them—but was that fair to Harry?

Neither of them had asked to be born into the life that they had. They were just two people whose lives had suddenly become intertwined.

She knew this wasn't destined to last forever. Harry was only here temporarily. But did she really want to ignore the spark between them? She'd gotten so used to only concentrating on work that she'd forgotten what it actually felt like to have a real connection with another human being. Someone to share with. Someone to have fun with.

And now? Now, she had one question to answer.

They were a million miles apart. But she'd never felt so close to someone in her life. She didn't need forever. She didn't need her perfect match.

But the electricity in the air was telling her what she needed, right here, right now.

She reached out her hand towards his. 'Yes,' she said clearly.

And as his hand closed over hers and pulled her towards him, the moment couldn't have been more perfect.

CHAPTER NINE

ALL OF A sudden he became part of the couple that the hospital had already believed existed.

It was amazing what quickly became normal.

He picked her up and took her back to his house. The immaculate town house became a little more rumpled.

A toothbrush appeared in the bathroom, along with shampoo, deodorant and a pink hairdryer.

Jeans were left over a chair in the bedroom. A small bag sat on the same chair filled with underwear.

Lemon marmalade and a certain brand of biscuits emerged in his kitchen cupboards. His long-ignored coffee machine took on a whole new lease of life. He'd lost the instruction manual ages ago, and could never remember all the functions that it took Esther less than five minutes to figure out.

He started to look for her constantly. In the canteen at work. In A&E. Every time he pushed open the doors to NICU—even when he knew she wasn't on shift.

No matter how many times he tried to persuade her otherwise, she wouldn't stop doing the occasional extra shift. She was proud, and needed the money for her family. It didn't matter that Harry could write her a cheque in seconds. It didn't matter that he wouldn't even miss the money from his bank account.

What mattered was that any conversation that went down that road could hurt Esther. Even when he bought her things—perfume, flowers, a book she wanted, a top she'd admired in a shop window—her first reaction was to bristle. Her second reaction was to tell him not to spend money on her.

For a woman who counted every penny and saved as much as she could, Esther was the least materialistic person he'd ever encountered.

He'd met his fair share of females in the past who knew exactly how wealthy he was, and were more than happy to accept gifts, holidays, even cars. The most forthright had left a catalogue from an exclusive jeweller's with a few items circled. The most expensive being an engagement ring that could take a baby's eye out with its sharp edges.

Esther was the opposite. She didn't want things. She didn't place value on things. She was happier with a written note, a card, a chocolate bar hidden under her pillow.

He had a sneaking feeling she resented his wealth a little. But it was a conversation they'd never had. It was like she'd drawn a line under it, accepted it, but was determined not to let it affect what happened between them.

Part of him was glad no one could ever label Esther as a potential gold-digger—that was a particular tabloid favourite. But part of him was sorry that she would be reluctant to accept any financial help that he might want to offer her. He tried to play it carefully because he respected her, and their relationship was still developing.

She'd even met a few of his friends. Penelope had drifted back into the background after sending him a few playful texts saying how much she liked Esther and she wanted to know when to buy a hat. Most of the friends he spent time with now were fellow surgeons, and Esther could more than match any of them.

It had taken a little pushing to get an introduction to Carly and Chloe, two fellow midwives she trusted. There was a third member of the quartet, Isabella, but she was apparently in New Zealand right now. He'd liked them both. Chloe had a cute kid that he'd entertained for more than an hour while the girls gossiped, but he'd liked that. He liked that Esther hadn't felt as if she constantly had to drag him into the conversation. She'd treated him like she expected him to be around for a long time, and this was something he should get used to. That sent a warm kind of glow around him that he hadn't expected.

Once they'd reached home they'd chatted as he made omelettes. Her phone had buzzed again. 'Your mum?' he asked.

She shook her head. 'Shirley, the A&E manager with an offer of shifts next week.'

'Don't,' he said, quicker than he meant to.

Her brow creased. 'What do you mean don't?'

It was too late to pull it back, but now was the time to say something that had been on his mind. 'You work every single day. We hardly ever get to spend time together. You know— like a normal couple. How about we have a day off together—a night off together where one, or both of us, doesn't have to get up at five in the morning to go into work.' He gave a sad kind of smile. 'Believe it or not, I actually like waking up next to you. How about we try and do it at least once a week?'

Her mouth was open, but she wasn't actually speaking. He had no idea what was currently spinning around in her mind. All he knew was his stomach was churning in case he'd just played this entirely wrong.

But Esther's eyes were on his, and the only thing he could see in them was warmth. 'A night falling asleep in each other's arms, and waking up the same way, could be kind of nice,' she said.

He moved around the counter towards her. 'It could,' he agreed.

She slipped her arm around his waist and smartly pulled his phone from his back pocket. 'Let me check your shifts. There's no point in me turning down these if you're already scheduled to work.'

He held his breath while she checked. She bit her bottom lip, then looked up at him. 'Okay, next Saturday. We'll have our first official day—and night—off together.'

He punched a fist into air. 'At last.'

Esther wasn't quite sure what came over her. She'd been so used to working seven days every week that the shock of taking one day off a week to spend with Harry felt like a permanent holiday.

She dined in some gorgeous restaurants; they attended the theatre together, went for long walks around some of the parks in London and enjoyed a private ride on the London Eye at night.

She tried hard to stop thinking about money all the time. That was her issue, not his.

But the best times were the ones where they just curled up on his sofa and watched TV. She was hardly spending any time in her own flat now. It seemed easier to stay at Harry's. A few of her possessions had taken up residence in his town house—her favourite cookbook, a framed photo with her mum and most of her clothes. Life felt like a fairy tale.

She'd gotten used to the stares at work, and the quiet whisperings. Hospitals were always the same. Next week, somebody else would be hospital news and she and Harry would just fade into the background.

In the meantime she was happy living a life that felt like part of a fairy tale.

She rubbed her eyes as she headed to the cash machine. Night shifts were never her favourite time. Every cell in her body protested to the wrench of its natural flow. She slid her card and blinked as she saw her balance. That couldn't be right.

She pressed a few other buttons. But the figure didn't change.

Her mouth went dry. There was a standard amount of money she always sent her mother and that would still be covered, but for the last few months, she'd managed to send an extra few hundred pounds because of all the shifts she covered. Her mother had never asked her for more. But Esther liked to do it.

This month, the money wasn't there. And she knew why.

Harry.

She leaned against the wall for a few minutes. She'd been turning down shifts on a regular basis. She still did one extra every week. But all of a sudden it didn't seem like enough.

Her stomach growled loudly and she walked to the vending machine to buy a sandwich, and stopped. She could do without. It wasn't like she'd fade away to nothing.

Her skin prickled. Her spending habits had changed in the last few weeks too. She'd stopped being so thrifty. She'd started heading to the canteen a few times a week instead of bagging her lunch. She didn't want him to pay for everything while they were out—even though he tried to insist. But those casual purchases of popcorn and coffee were all adding up. None of this was Harry's fault, but somehow, being around him had made her forget her priorities.

It was time she had a rethink.

She pulled her phone from her pocket, returning a text Shirley had sent earlier offering shifts in A&E. She said yes to them all.

Then she texted the agency too. There was

still one day this month where she could squeeze in an extra shift.

Her eyes caught sight of a text from earlier. Harry. Wishing you were here with me tonight. See you in the morning. She smiled and stuck the phone back in her pocket. She'd need to talk to him at some point.

Harry would be fine. He'd understand.

He was already sleeping when his phone rang.

His eyes narrowed at the name on the screen. 'Penelope?'

'Hey, Harry, sorry if I've woken you.' Her voice sounded a little shaky, not the self-assured way it normally was. Harry sat upright in bed.

'What's wrong?'

He heard her take a few slow breaths. 'Penelope?'

'I'm sorry, this was silly. I'll be fine. I shouldn't have called.'

All of his senses were on alert. 'Penelope. Tell me what's wrong.'

He suddenly realised that whilst her voice was low—as if she were whispering into the phone—there was also a slight echo around it. 'Where are you?'

She named a well-known venue in London. 'I came here with Lance Derby.'

Harry rolled his eyes. Lance wasn't his favourite. A banker who was arrogant and opinionated. 'And?'

'He's had a bit too much to drink—we both have, really—and…'

Her voice tailed off. Harry swung his legs out of bed. 'And what?'

'He's been more than a bit forward with me.'

'What do you mean?' Harry was already on his feet, looking for his clothes.

Penelope let out a noise that sounded like a sob.

Her voice cracked. 'I'm sorry, Harry. I feel like some kind of teenager. I shouldn't be calling you.'

'Whereabouts are you at the club?' he asked as he pulled his T-shirt over his head.

'In the bathroom,' came the whisper.

He stopped. 'You're in the bathroom?'

'It's the only place I feel safe,' she admitted. 'I know he's waiting outside the door. I've heard him shouting at a few people. He wants to take me home, and I just don't want to go back out there. Not when he's drunk like this. I… I'm not sure what he thinks taking me home means.'

Harry's mind had already been made up a few minutes ago. 'I'll be there as soon as I can.'

There was an audible breath of relief, then Penelope added, 'But, Harry, I'm not sure they'll let you in. It was an invite-only event tonight.'

Something clicked in Harry's brain. He walked to his dresser and rummaged through the mail lying on top. 'I think I had one of those. Give me a sec.' He pulled an envelope out from the stack. 'Yes, I've got it.'

He glanced at his reflection in the mirror and realised that joggers and a T-shirt wouldn't gain him entry to the exclusive members club. 'Okay, don't move. I'm changing and I'll be with you shortly. If you feel safe in the ladies', then stay there. Don't move.'

He changed into a suit, shirt and tie in record time and jumped into his car. Thankfully the streets of London were much quieter at this time of night and it didn't take him long to reach the venue.

He waved his invitation and stepped inside. Sure enough, Lance Derby was pacing outside the ladies' bathrooms. Harry did his best not to grit his teeth but the sensations were pretty much overwhelming. Lance wasn't just drunk, he was very drunk, loud and obnoxious.

He walked towards Lance, who'd started to talk loudly to another male guest, telling him exactly what he was waiting for.

Harry didn't hesitate. He grabbed Lance by the scruff of the neck and the seat of his pants, practically lifting him from the floor as he marched him back to the front door. One of the members of staff visibly gulped, panic on her face.

Lance started to try and wrestle his way from Harry's grip, but his drunken moves were uncoordinated and his shouts slurred.

'Get off me, get off me.' He turned his head and caught a glimpse of Harry. 'Oh, it's you,' he said in a mocking voice. 'The white knight. Well, get lost, Harry. You had your chance. Penelope's coming home with me.'

He was still trying to struggle as Harry nodded to one of the staff to open the front door. Several people had come to some of the doors of the club and were watching every movement. This could be dangerous. Harry had spotted a few paparazzi at the end of the street. There were obviously a few events going on in the same area of London tonight. He paused at the entrance way. 'Is there a cab outside?'

The doorman took a quick glance and waved his arm. 'Just a moment, sir.'

Lance kept wrestling, but Harry's grip was strong.

The doorman gave a nod. 'Can you open the door for me?' asked Harry.

A few seconds later there was a shout from outside. 'Ready!'

Harry bundled Lance down the steps and straight into the empty cab, thrusting some money towards the driver and rattling off Lance's address. He'd known him long enough to know exactly where he lived.

He waited a few moments as the cab drove off, then straightened his suit and walked back inside.

He knocked on the door of the ladies' and waited a few moments before gently pushing it open.

'Pen? Are you here? It's Harry. Lance is gone. I've put him in a cab and sent him home.'

The door to one of the panelled wooden stalls opened and Penelope walked unsteadily out, her face streaked with tears. She collapsed into Harry's arms. 'I'm so sorry to phone you. Say sorry to Esther too. It's the middle of the night.'

Harry shook his head. 'It's fine, and Esther's working. Even if she hadn't been, she would have been fine with me coming for you.'

He took a deep breath. 'Did he touch you? Did he do anything to you?'

Penelope shook her head. She didn't meet Harry's eyes. 'It didn't get that far. He just got drunker and drunker and told me exactly what he expected later. That was enough. I thought I could just duck away, but when I came to the bathroom, he started hanging around outside.' Her voice was trembling. 'And I wasn't sure who would have my back if I'd gone outside again.'

Harry trembled as he kept his rage buttoned up inside. He put his hands ever so gently on Penelope's face. 'No one should ever make you feel like that. No one should ever make you feel unsafe. I'll always have your back, Pen. Know that. Know that always. Any time, day or night, that you don't feel safe, you can call me. That's what friends are for.'

Her eyes finally met his and he could feel her whole body sag in relief. She put her hand over his. 'I'm just glad you were able to come and get me.' She took a long, slow breath. 'Would you mind taking me home?'

'Of course not.'

She nodded, then turned to the mirror. 'Give me a second.'

She cleaned up her face and combed her hair, rapidly looking more like the polished Penelope the world normally viewed. He gave her a few moments while she put her hands on either side of the sink and did some deep breathing.

'Ready,' said Penelope, sounding a little more like normal. 'Thank you,' she said again. 'I'm sorry to phone in the middle of the night. But I just knew I needed some help—and you were the first person I knew I could count on.'

He gave her a thoughtful nod. 'Any time, Penelope. Any time you need help, just pick up the phone.'

She slid her hand into Harry's arm as they walked outside towards Harry's car.

'Duke, Penelope,' came a shout nearby.

They turned automatically as a camera flashed. Harry shook his head as he opened the car door for her. 'Sorry about that. I'd seen them, but thought they were at the club down the street.'

'No probs,' said Penelope as she fastened her seat belt. 'Just get me home. I can't wait for this night to be over.'

Esther's phone rang, sending a jolt through the staff who were currently sitting at the nursing station in NICU. Her heart missed a few beats when she saw the name on the screen. *Mum.*

She automatically stood up, stepping away from her colleagues towards the back wall of NICU. 'Mum, what's wrong? Is everything all right?'

She froze. The voice at the end of the phone wasn't her mother's. It was one of the neighbours.

'Esther, I'm so sorry to phone you at this time. It's Gladys. There's been a bit of an issue here.'

'Where's my mum? Is she okay?'

There was a long intake of breath. 'Yes, yes, I think so. They've just taken her away in the ambulance. A bit of smoke inhalation, but they think she'll be okay. I'm just going to follow the ambulance but she wanted me to phone you first.'

'Smoke inhalation? What's happened?' She couldn't keep her voice quiet right now. All heads in the unit turned towards her.

'I'm so sorry, honey, but the house…it's gone up in flames. The fire brigade are here now. They have no idea how things started and they think they have the blaze under control, but—to be honest, Esther—your mum can't go back there. The roof is damaged, the kitchen…' She let her voice tail off.

Esther sagged back against the wall just for a second as she blinked back tears.

'I'm coming. I'm on my way.' She brushed the tears from her face. 'Tell her I'll be there as soon as I can.'

She finished the call as her colleagues surrounded her, instantly asking if they could help.

'I'll cover your patients.'

'We can arrange some emergency leave.'

'Do you want me to go online and book the first flight for you?'

She nodded as she tried to collect her thoughts. 'Harry,' she said in a low voice. 'I should phone Harry.'

Two of her colleagues exchanged glances.

'Maybe not,' said the one that was usually more bolshie.

Esther shook her head. 'Why?'

There was an awkward pause, then one of them took her phone from her pocket and pulled up the Twitter feed for one of the daily rags. *Has the Duke Found His Bride?* was the headline of just over an hour ago.

The picture that accompanied it was of Harry, dressed in a suit with his arm around Penelope, looking her usual glamorous self. Harry looked worried—was that because he knew his picture was being taken? But Penelope didn't look worried at all. She had her hand on the front of Harry's chest and was looking at him like Harry was some kind of saviour. Esther's stomach twisted into a knot.

Harry had texted earlier and said he was in bed. Alone.

The text from earlier must have been a lie and that made her stomach clench in anger and humiliation.

Because this picture showed something entirely different. And the way that Penelope was looking at him…made her wonder if she'd missed something completely. Could that be love? Adoration?

Whatever it was it made her want to be sick all over her shoes and punch a wall.

Nothing like being humiliated in front of the world.

'I'm sorry, honey,' said Caroline, one of her older colleagues. 'But you've enough to deal with right now. Concentrate on your mum. Anything else can wait.'

It was clear she could tell that the tears forming in Esther's eyes were a mixture of things.

Esther trusted Caroline. She'd never steered her wrong in the past. Caroline put her arm around her shoulders. 'Get your things. I'll walk you down and see if we can get you a cab.'

Esther's mind was swirling. She didn't know what to think. Anger was racing through her veins. What she really wanted to do was dial his number and scream and shout. But grabbing some things and getting to the airport was so much more important right now.

And even though she knew that, it didn't stop the horrible aching of her heart, or the hurt at the apparent betrayal.

But there was something else. Even if this hadn't happened. Part of her knew that depending what she found when she got back to Scotland, she might never come back here. She had to put her mum's needs first—because she was all she had.

She tilted her chin upwards defiantly. Maybe this was all for the best. The end for the two of them was inevitable. It had just happened sooner than she'd expected. She'd been too trusting. She'd had her head in the clouds.

She'd lived the Cinderella fairy tale for too long.

And everyone knew that fairy tales weren't real.

CHAPTER TEN

HARRY WOKE EARLY—even though he'd had very little sleep.

Penelope had managed to gather herself by the time he'd taken her home. She was starting to get angry, and he didn't blame her.

He was glad she'd called. Glad he'd been able to help her out. He knew he would do it again in a heartbeat.

But coming home to an empty bed made him feel odd. He'd gotten so used to having Esther here that now it seemed off when she wasn't. He loved the heat from her body and the way her skin seemed to mould against his.

Waking up now made the town house just feel…empty.

He froze.

Empty had been pretty much how his life had felt for a long time. It wasn't just that he didn't form relationships with other people; it was just that he had been brought up that way. It wasn't the norm for him.

He'd never opened up to another person the way he had with Esther. He'd never shared with someone else the way he had with Esther. Of course he had friends, colleagues and a scattered extended family.

But who was really there to think about him? To consider him?

He thought back to the night he'd received the call about his father. Regret swamped him. He couldn't pretend he hadn't almost hated his father. But, as an adult, he regretted the opportunity that he'd missed to have one final talk. His father had collapsed and died quickly. He hadn't had some painful disease. There had been no suffering. Harry had thought the old man might actually have lived until he was a hundred.

But the last few weeks, seeing the strong relationship Esther had with her mother filled him with regret. His father might have always remained an opinionated, self-centred, hateful man. Or maybe, if he'd been ill or sick, there might have been some regrets.

And that's what left Harry with a hole in his heart. There was no sense of closure. He wished he'd driven down to the country estate at least one time in the five years before his father had died. Even if it had resulted in yet another fight, it might have made him feel a little more sure about his complete avoidance of his father in the last few years of his life.

Maybe it was just his own idea of a fairy tale—that his father would have lived to regret the wasted years between them. The way he'd treated Harry, the way he'd ignored him. That there could have been some last-minute kind of reconciliation. He'd spent his life feeling so isolated. So alone.

Being around Esther had broken down a whole host of barriers he'd spent his life reinforcing. She challenged him. She excited him. She celebrated and commiserated with him. When he sat on the sofa at night now, he didn't feel comfortable unless she was perched alongside him.

It hadn't even been that long, and maybe he was crazy, but it felt like his life had changed immeasurably.

She was helping him fill out the little parts of himself that had always felt as if they were missing. The parts that his parents had stolen from him, and he'd never had a chance to steal back.

Seeing her relationship with her mother had taught him it was all right to have regrets about how things had turned out with his father. There had never been a good relationship between him and his father in the first place. But that didn't mean he hadn't secretly wished for it. He would have loved to have the kind of relationship with his dad that Esther had with her mum. The love, the mutual respect—even the genuine interest in each other—was something he'd spent most of life yearning for, just not letting himself admit to. He'd never allowed himself to feel that way before. He could now wish things had been different—even if it was much too late. It didn't make him weak. It just made him human.

She would be finishing at work soon. If he got ready and left now, he could meet her with her favourite coffee before she left for home— his home.

Their home.

He swallowed. He hadn't asked her yet.

He'd been letting the idea float around his brain for a few days while he got comfortable with it.

No, actually, that was a lie. He was comfortable with it as soon as it first got there. But what he didn't want to do was scare her off and send her running for the hills.

Was it normal to ask someone if they wanted to move in permanently after a few short weeks?

For the first time in his life Harry had found something he wanted to keep hold of. Found something he wanted to build and nurture. Last thing he wanted to do was ask the question and watch her squirm as she struggled to find a way to say no.

He also had a secret to tell her that could help their budding relationship.

His brain played with the thoughts all the way to the Queen Victoria. He noticed his hand was trembling as he paid for the coffee and it made him smile.

He liked these nerves. They felt like good nerves. Maybe asking Esther to move in with him after a night shift wasn't the best idea on the planet—he could probably time it better, arrange a more romantic setting than the hospital entrance—but all he knew was he didn't want to wait.

He wanted to ask her now. Ask her while things felt so good between them, so right.

He glanced at his watch. The shift handover was taking longer than normal. He'd just go on up to NICU. He had patients to check on anyway.

He swung the doors open with a cheery 'Good morning,' only to be met by silence.

He strode across the entrance way and sat the coffee cups down on the desk. 'Where's Esther?' he asked. He knew who she'd been working with last night and the rest of the staff was still there.

One of the older midwives closest to him sucked in her breath through her teeth. Another midwife shot him a dagger-like glare. Two others just pointedly ignored him as if he hadn't spoken at all.

He turned to the woman beside him. 'Caroline, what's going on—is Esther okay?'

Caroline pressed her lips together for a few seconds as panic started to grip at his chest. He could tell she was considering what to tell him. She kept her voice low. 'She got a call last night from her mother. It was an emergency. There was a fire at her mother's house and she had to go back to Scotland.'

'What?' He nearly dropped the coffee that he'd picked back up. He yanked his phone from his pocket. 'But she would have called, she would have texted.' He stared at the blank screen.

Another voice cut in behind him. 'Hey, you, Mr Flighty, my office, now.' The thick Irish accent was curt.

He turned around to face Oona, shaking his head. 'No, I can't. I need to talk to Esther.'

The small, burly woman stepped closer, barely an inch from his face. 'It wasn't a request.'

Harry was taken aback, his fingers already pressing the buttons on his phone to dial Esther, but he followed her into her office, watching in bewilderment as she closed the door with a kick.

Oona folded her arms across her chest. 'Don't bet on Esther answering your calls.'

'What?' He looked up from his phone screen.

'After your shenanigans last night, I doubt she'll talk to you again.'

He frowned as a text beeped on his phone. Penelope. He could see the first line of the text. *Oh no.*

He shook his head as he tried to work out what on earth was going on. 'What...shenanigans?' He didn't even like saying the word. *Harry* and *shenanigans* had never been in the same sentence before.

Oona waved one hand. 'Had a good night, did you?'

He wrinkled his brow. 'What?'

She gave him a hard stare. 'You're looking remarkably fresh for someone who was out until two in the morning.'

Something prickled at the back of his brain—and it wasn't good.

'How do you know that?'

She gave him a look of disgust. 'The whole world knows that, Harry. If you're going to play away, have the decency not to be so public about it.'

He took a deep breath. 'I have no idea what you're talking about.' He resisted the temptation to pull up the rest of Penelope's message.

Oona's look of disgust stayed firmly in place. 'I'd like to use words that would be deemed "unprofessional," so I won't. But this is my unit, my NICU, Harry, and I expect my staff to be treated with respect. Maybe no one warned you about mixing business with pleasure, but when things get messy like this, the atmosphere can affect everyone who is in here. Staff, patients and relatives. Humiliating a member of my staff in public is hardly going to result in an atmosphere for babies that's conducive to healing, is it?'

He was beginning to get mad. Esther's phone was just ringing out. Perhaps she was on the plane?

'Why don't you explain exactly what you think I've done, Oona, and stop speaking in riddles.'

She gritted her teeth and pulled her phone from her tunic, turning it to face him. 'You— and your apparent potential bride—are all over social media since the early hours, after falling out of some club together. And yes. Esther's seen it. Which is why I doubt very much she'll answer any of your calls.' Oona shook her head. 'You really couldn't have timed this any worse.'

Dread swept over him. The headline above the photo of him and Penelope was bad enough.

Will Penelope Brackenridge Be the New Duchess of Montrose?

But the photo certainly didn't help. It looked... kind of compromising, even from his gaze. It didn't matter that he knew what had happened. It didn't matter that he knew there was absolutely nothing in it. He knew exactly what the press were like. And his heart sunk at the thought of Esther being confronted with this last night in the midst of the bad news from back home.

He straightened his back and looked Oona straight in the eye. 'That picture is not what you think. Penelope is my friend, has been since we were five. She phoned me last night when she felt threatened. I picked her up and took her home.' Anger was rising in him. He didn't need to give Oona an explanation of his behaviour, but he wanted to—for Esther's sake. At least Oona had been up front with him; now he knew exactly what was going on and why Esther hadn't answered his calls. He turned to walk away. He had things to sort; he needed to find cover for today, and probably tomorrow too. Then he'd need to try and find a flight.

His hand was on the doorknob when he turned back around. It was like every little light had taken fire in his brain at once. He could explain this to Esther, of course he could. But more than that, he wanted to be by her side. She'd be devastated over what had happened back in Scotland and he didn't want her to go through that alone. She shouldn't have to, and she didn't need to.

He turned back to Oona. 'Just so you know, I would do it again—in a heartbeat—for any friend, male or female, who told me they felt unsafe.' Then his expression softened. 'And why on earth would anyone think that I'd cheat on Esther—the woman that I love?'

He watched as Oona's eyes widened as he stepped out of the office and picked up the phone. He had no surgeries scheduled in the next few days, but a couple of babies who would require surgery when delivered. He made sure his contact details were available for the responsible hospitals as he knew that even with the best-laid plans, babies sometimes had ideas of their own.

Francesca appeared at his side. 'You okay?'

'No,' he said honestly. 'But I will be.'

She didn't ask questions, just gave his arm a squeeze. 'You know you can leave any instructions with me.'

He pulled his notes from a pad. 'And I was just doing that.' He gave her a hug. 'Thank you for this, and phone me if there's anything at all.'

She nodded slowly and pressed her lips together. 'I'll try my best not to.'

He wasn't worried about the hushed atmosphere around him now. Oona would spread the news in his absence, and gossip like this would fly through the hospital like a firework.

He'd just declared his love for Esther.

He hadn't even known until that second that he was going to say those words.

But right now, he needed to tell them to the person who mattered most.

And that was exactly what he planned to do.

CHAPTER ELEVEN

SHE COULD ALMOST swear that her heart hadn't stopped racing in her chest until that moment that she finally saw her mother lying in the hospital bed and rushed over to wrap her arms around her.

Finally, she could breathe.

She was here. She was alive.

It didn't matter that her mother was lying in a hospital bed with crisp white sheets, or that she was wearing a pale blue hospital gown. As Esther encompassed her in a hug, all she could smell was the smoke. It clung to her mother's hair and skin, with even a smudge of something on her cheek.

Esther tried to hold back her tears. It wouldn't do for her mum to see her so upset. She sat at the edge of the bed—ignoring all the rules that said she shouldn't—and took both of her mum's hands.

'I am so glad you're safe. What happened?'

Her mum didn't speak for a few moments. 'I'm not sure. I was in bed. I think it might have been the washing machine. That's what the fire officer said. One minute I was sleeping, and the next the place was full of smoke.' Her voice was trembling now. 'I just grabbed my slippers and dressing gown and ran down the stairs.' She shook her head. 'My bag was sitting on the table near the front door so I grabbed it too on my way out.' Her eyes were filled with tears. 'I couldn't even go near the sitting room.' She shivered. 'The heat coming out of there was too much.'

Esther couldn't hide the fact that she was shaking too. She'd seen too much in A&E, saw the impact of house fires. Helped when trying to resuscitate adults and children who'd been overcome by smoke. Knowing that one of those people could have been her mother was just too much.

She hugged her again tightly. 'Oh, I'm so glad you woke up. I'm so glad you ran.'

Her mother bowed her head, holding on tight to her. Esther knew her mum was just as glad to see her. She must have got such a fright last night. 'You didn't need to come all this way,' her mum whispered. 'I'm so sorry. You're so busy. And you've got so much to do. You shouldn't need to worry about me.'

Esther put her hand on her mother's cheek.

'I'll *always* worry about you. You're my number one priority.'

Her mother's voice stayed low. 'But you shouldn't be doing that. You should be out living your own life, having fun.'

Something twisted inside Esther. She didn't like the way this conversation was going. She knew her mother too well.

When she was stressed about something, she tried to find a way to say words without actually having to say them. Just like she was doing now.

She'd already told her mum that she was dating someone—she just hadn't filled in all the blanks. But it didn't feel like this was where this was going.

'What is it, Mum? Just tell me.'

Her mum's eyes brimmed with tears. 'I don't think you'll be able to stay in the house. There'll be too much damage. Gladys says you can stay with her tonight.'

'Don't worry about me. Let me sort things out. I'll arrange to get the house cleaned up, and the place assessed. I'll contact the insurers. Just you rest. Worry about getting better. Let me worry about everything else.'

Harry had only been standing outside the small fire-damaged house for a few minutes when one of the neighbours approached. 'Are you looking for Mrs McDonald?' she asked.

He nodded. 'And Esther—I'm looking for her daughter too.'

The woman glanced back at the house and shuddered. 'Come with me. Esther will be staying at mine tonight. I'm sure she'll be back once she's done with visiting at the hospital. Let me make you some tea.'

He'd barely blinked before a large teapot appeared, along with an eclectic array of mugs and a plate of biscuits and thick wedges of fruit loaf.

'I'm Gladys,' the woman said, sitting at the other side of the table. She gave Harry the eye, in the way that a woman of a certain age only could. 'Are you Esther's young man?'

He wasn't quite sure how to answer that one. He wanted to be. He wanted to be more than her young man, but until he'd spoken to Esther it didn't seem fair to introduce himself that way.

He stretched his hand across the table. 'I'm Harry, Esther's friend. We work together.'

Gladys's eyebrows lifted. 'From what I hear, that's the only way to see Esther these days.'

He nodded in agreement. 'She works very hard.'

Gladys opened her mouth as if she were about to say something else, then stopped, giving a simple nod. 'She does.'

The doorbell rang and Esther walked through the door. 'Harry.' She stood frozen in shock. She looked tired out, her skin pale and her eyes dark.

Her gaze flitted between Harry and Gladys. 'How…?'

'Here.' Gladys jumped up. 'Have some tea. You look like you need it. I need to pop to the corner shop. So now that you're back, I'll leave you and Harry for five minutes.'

Within a few seconds Gladys was gone but Esther still stood frozen on the spot. Harry stood up and stepped over. He tentatively lifted an arm to put around her shoulders but stopped as she flinched.

'Don't touch me.' She thudded her bag down on the table. 'And what on earth are you doing here?' Angry tears were flooding her eyes and he hated that this was his fault.

'Nothing happened. You must know that, Esther.'

'Really? All I know is that you told me you were spending the night in bed when you were actually falling out of a club in London with Penelope!' Her words cut in before he had a chance to add anything.

Her hands were on the table, her body leaning over towards him, and he could see her whole body was shaking.

'How's your mum?'

'What?' She seemed taken aback by his question. Then she stopped and took a breath. 'My mum is okay. Smoke inhalation. Because of her frailty, they've kept her in. She'll get reassessed tomorrow.'

She sagged down onto the chair behind her and he poured her some tea. There was so much he wanted to say, so much he wanted to rush in with, but this wasn't about him. It was about her.

Her hands were still trembling as she picked up the mug. 'Tea.' She grimaced.

'I didn't like to ask Gladys if she had any coffee,' he added, but his light-hearted tone seemed off.

She didn't even look at him. Just closed her eyes and leaned her head on one hand. 'I can't even see the house until later when the fire chief comes back. I don't even know if anything is salvageable—if the house is even salvageable.'

Every part of him ached for her. He took a breath, knowing how these words might sound. 'It's only a house, Esther. You've still got your mum and she's doing okay.'

She sobbed into her hand. 'I know that. I know that. When I got to the hospital I just remembered every patient I've ever treated who'd been involved in a house fire. I couldn't even breathe just thinking about it.'

He winced. He knew exactly what she meant.

The way that smoke lingered in the air of the department after they'd been treated. The horrible charcoal-like smell of burning skin. It was one of the hardest things to deal with, and for Esther to think that might have been her mum...

He stood back up and walked around the table, this time not giving her opportunity to flinch. This time just pulling her up to him and hugging her to his chest.

She didn't fight it. She just slowly wrapped her arms around his waist and stayed there. He wasn't sure how long they stood. Much longer than the five minutes that Gladys said she'd be.

When she finally pulled her face back from his chest she just shook her head. 'What are you doing here, Harry? Why did you come?'

The furrows in her brow were deep and her eyes littered with confusion.

'Why do you think I came? I came because I love you, Esther, and I didn't want you to be alone.'

Her muscles tensed and she stepped back, holding out her hands.

'But that picture. The lies you told me...'

'No. I told you the truth. I was in my bed. But Penelope phoned and she was in trouble. She'd gone out with someone who'd made her feel threatened. She was drunk and asked if I'd come and get her.'

Esther blinked, no words coming out. 'What?' It was barely a whisper.

He bent down towards her. 'You know there's nothing between Penelope and me. It's just not like that. I love her like a sister, and in a way, I wish she was, at least then I'd have a family that was worth caring about.'

She stepped back and sat back down. When she looked at him again with those big blue eyes he sensed something from her. It was time for truths.

She put her hands on the table. 'Are you going to tell me about your father? Your parents?'

He spoke honestly. It was the only way he could do this. 'I was part of a family that my sole purpose was to be the heir. There was really no other requirement. Neither of my parents was interested in having a child. They just saw it as their duty.'

Esther just looked confused. 'Who looked after you at home? What about school holidays? Surely you spent some time with them? They spent all your time ignoring you?' She was shaking her head as if she really couldn't get her head around it.

He stayed patient for a moment. Then took a deep breath. 'Esther, you seem like a girl who spent her childhood surrounded by love. It was normal for you. It wasn't normal for me.' He put his hand to his chest. 'I thought what I had was normal. I thought it was normal to have parents who didn't look at you when you entered the room. Who didn't care how you were, or how you felt. I spent my life being brought up by an ever-changing rota of nannies. Most of them left before I ever really got to know them. There was one maid who worked in my parents' house for seven years—she was the only person who ever laughed and joked with me. I went to boarding school. I rarely saw other kids interact with their parents, so I thought that what I had was entirely normal.' He felt his own voice start to break, so he stopped talking.

Esther sat with her eyes wide. As if she were taking everything in and processing it.

Harry breathed again. He was here to tell her that he loved her. He wanted her to move in with him. To take a chance on him. He had to let her know exactly what she was getting.

He tightened his grip on her hand. 'But I'm not crazy. I know that is ridiculous. But everything about my relationship with them—my parents—coloured every part of my life. It's hard to learn to love, to share with someone, when you've never had an example of that to learn from. I didn't see it every day. That's why you're so important to me, Esther.' He looked over and met her blue gaze. 'You're the first person I've met that I've found it easy to love.'

Her mug clattered against the table. He'd said it three times now. Once to Oona, and twice to Esther. She seemed to be listening, but was she hearing?

Her fingers tightened around the mug. 'Why?'

He gave a slow nod. She wanted to know it all. 'Because you never asked me for anything. You didn't want me for anything.' He gave a gentle smile. 'You didn't even like me to begin with. Then I started being around you. I could see the relationship you had with your patients and their families. I could see how you worked hard in amongst your colleagues. And you could adapt, you could work anywhere—' his gaze met hers '—because you felt you had to.'

'And that makes me easy to love?'

'Sure it does. Because it's all about how big your heart is, and how much you love. Your only agenda is looking after your mum. Making sure she's okay.' He paused for a second, wondering if he should actually say these words out loud.

'And the worst part is that even though I know they ignored me, I spent years witnessing it. Deep down, I still wanted them to love me. When my father dropped dead, I realised that was it. It was all over. There would never be any kind of shot at redemption. I'd never get to sit at the side of my dying father's bed and listen to him apologise for how he'd treated me, and tell me that he did actually love me. I shut all those thoughts and possibilities out.'

'Oh, Harry, why?' She sounded incredulous.

'Because I wanted to be loved. I wanted to feel worthy of being loved. I wanted parents who would be proud of me. Just like your parents did. People look at me and think, *He's rich, he's got everything.* But I never had an iota of what you had. I've spent my life keeping my distance from people. Not letting my guard down. Because letting your guard down means you can get hurt.' His voice broke a little. 'And you're the only person I've felt able to do that with. I love watching what you have with your mum. The two of you are as close as can be. You talk all the time. You have pictures of your mum, and dad, all around your flat. And in those pictures? You're all in each other's arms, wrapped around each other.' He paused again, his voice hoarse. 'You've no idea how much I wish I'd had the same normal as you. And up until now, I've never admitted that. Not to anyone. Not even to myself.'

She blinked, her eyes wet, and as soon as he saw that he immediately wanted to take back all the parts of himself he'd exposed.

He straightened in his chair. 'I was never abused. I was never cold, never hungry. I didn't want for anything, really, apart from love and somebody to show some interest in me.'

'That doesn't make it right,' she said bluntly. 'We see the worst of some families in the health service. Being fed, clothed and having a roof over your head doesn't mean you didn't suffer from neglect. That sounds exactly like what happened.' She moved from her chair at the other side of the table over next to him. Her gentle floral scent following her across the room. It was all he could do not to breathe in and inhale it strongly.

'You swept me up in a fairy tale,' she said, the edges of her voice a little sad. 'I wasn't looking for a prince, or a duke, but I found one anyway.'

His hands moved to her waist. 'And is that good, or bad?'

'Both,' she said without qualm as she sat down in his lap. 'You know, you're making assumptions. I have an almost great relationship with my mother, but it's not perfect. Not the way you think. Do you know she didn't tell me straight away about the cancer?'

'What?' Harry was surprised.

She shook her head sadly. 'She didn't tell me straight away because she didn't want me to worry, about her, and the fact she couldn't manage to work any more. She didn't want to put the responsibility on to me. I was really hurt when I found out.' She stopped for a second and swallowed. 'But I understood she did it out of love.'

She took another breath. 'And my dad wasn't perfect. I admit, I loved and adored him. But as a child I didn't realise how his flyaway behaviour put extra pressure on my mum to be the foundation of the family. To try and hold down more than one job.' She put her hand to her chest. 'It's affected me more than I've ever realised.'

She took a few moments to speak, and when she looked at him again her eyes were filled with sorrow. 'But how can I leave now I've come back to find this? I can't walk away from my mum when everything is in such a state.'

It was like someone switching a light on in his brain. Even though she'd been mad at him for the photo—even though she hadn't really understood the context—it hadn't been the most important thing to her.

He'd seen how damaged the house was. It could take months to fix—if it could be fixed. Esther had already made up her mind that she needed to stay to support her mother. She had no intention of coming back to London.

He looked at her as his breath caught halfway up his throat. He hadn't even considered this—and to anyone that knew Esther, this was obvious.

'We can find a way to work things out,' he said determinedly.

'How? You in London, me up here?' She shook her head. 'That's crazy. We both know it is.'

There was a loud knock at the door and Gladys came back in, a shopping bag clasped in one hand, and a large man at her shoulder.

'Esther,' she said apologetically. 'The fire guy is here. He said he can let you collect a few things from the house.'

'Let me help,' said Harry as he grabbed his jacket.

For a second he thought she might refuse, but then she gave a little nod of her head. 'Okay.'

Her voice was cracking again; as she headed out in front of him, Harry hoped it wouldn't be the last word he would hear from her.

Five minutes later Esther had a hard hat on her head and some strict instructions from the fire guy. They'd had a quick chat about things she would really like to retrieve from the house and where they might be. Part of the roof was dangerous and was a complete no-go area, along with the kitchen.

'Brace yourself,' the guy said. 'The inside of the sitting room is completely smoke-damaged.'

Harry's face had remained steady. He put his

hand on her shoulder as they went through the front door and she was glad to have it there.

The acrid smell of smoke burned her throat as she stepped inside. It seemed that even though many of the items of furniture in her mother's house met with the newer fire regulations, there had still been a few older pieces that had burned to a crisp. Amazingly, her mother's old heavy curtains were entirely intact, even though they were blackened by the fumes.

Harry moved quickly, picking up the photos she'd asked him to from the mantelpiece and the walls. Esther pulled open a cupboard under the stairs and retrieved the box with all the documentation they would need with her mother's bank details and different policies. Next were some photo albums, and a few more sentimental pieces.

'What about upstairs?' she asked.

'Which side of the house?' asked the fire officer.

Esther pointed. He nodded. 'Okay, I'll send one of my team up. That side is unaffected but I'd still rather it wasn't you. Tell me what you need.'

A few minutes later she had most of her mother's clothes and shoes in boxes. The majority of the items had very little obvious smoke damage as they'd been sealed inside an old-fashioned wardrobe. It was likely, with a quick laundry, her mother's clothes would be fine.

Esther gave a sigh of relief. 'I think that should be everything for now.'

The fire officer nodded. 'We need to make the house secure in the meantime until repairs are done. You might not get back in here for a while.'

She gave a tearful nod. This was the house where she'd grown up, created all the memories that Harry was so envious of. But that's all they were. Memories. She still had her mum, and she needed to make sure she got things sorted out. As she picked up the last few things she wanted to take with her she was overwhelmed with sadness.

Of course she was going to do this for her mother. But part of her heart ached in sadness over Harry. He'd kept a stoic look in place as she'd told him that she couldn't come back to London, and she would never ask him to give up anything for her. She had to. Of course she had to.

When he'd told her exactly how things had been for him as a child all she'd wanted to do was run over and wrap him in her arms. But what would that achieve? Twice she'd heard him use the words that made her heart want to swell with joy. She couldn't let herself respond. She couldn't tell him that he'd completely and utterly stolen her heart too. Not when she had to tell him she wasn't coming home.

The word was like an arrow through her heart. *Home.* That's what Harry's house felt like. Not her own flat back in London—it had never felt like home. But the town house? It felt like home because Harry was there. Every association she had with that place revolved around him. Him lying in the bed beside her. Her slumping in his arms on the sofa. Him cooking eggs and pancakes in the kitchen, sometimes for breakfast, sometimes late at night. If she stood in the town house and breathed in, she could smell him, because Harry smelled like home to her now.

'Hey? Okay?' He'd walked over and slipped an arm around her shoulders, obviously thinking she was upset about the house, and not the person who was standing next to her.

She blinked back the tears. She had to. Her heart was still aching for him. She wanted to tell him that she loved him too. But how could she do that when she couldn't see any way for them to be together now? She'd have to start looking for jobs. Anything would do. There was a nursing home nearby; she could try them first. It wouldn't be the same salary she'd be getting in London, but it was somewhere to start.

She shook the hand of the fire officer. 'Thank

you.' Right now, as much as she loved this place in the past, she couldn't wait to get back outside.

She walked quickly back down to Gladys's house. Harry put a hand on her shoulder. 'How about I go and find us some coffee?'

She nodded and pressed her lips together. It was almost like he knew she needed a few moments alone.

She started going through the box of documents. The sooner she started to deal with things, the better. But the first phone call to the insurance company made her stomach plummet.

'What? What do you mean?' She listened, thinking that the woman at the end of the phone was clearly from another planet. 'Not paid. When? That can't be right?'

Her mother's bank statements were neatly filed in a little folder. Esther started to flick rapidly through them, finding all the direct debits and swallowing as she saw the bank balance, and that some had been refused.

This couldn't be happening. Please no. Not now.

She listened for a few more moments. The woman at the end of the phone was being lovely, but quite clear. As soon as the payments had defaulted, letters had been sent. There was a thirty-day window to make good on the payment, and then the policy was void.

She replaced the receiver in shock.

'What is it?' Gladys asked.

Esther glanced at the clock. The conversation had lasted more than an hour, but it felt as if it had gone by in the blink of an eye.

'Sh-she has no insurance.' Esther's voice came out choked and half audible.

To her surprise, Gladys just gave a little nod of her head and sat down opposite her.

'But I was sending her money. The last few weeks I hadn't managed to work quite as many shifts, but I still sent her the same amount she'd always needed. I just couldn't add any extra.'

Gladys's face was sympathetic but tight. 'Costs go up, Esther. The shopping, the gas, the electricity. The council tax went up here a couple of months ago.'

'What? She didn't tell me that.'

Gladys met her gaze. 'She didn't want to. She thought you were putting too much on yourself already. She didn't want you to make yourself unwell.' Gladys sighed. 'She also thought you weren't giving yourself any chance of a life.' She shot Esther a sympathetic glance. 'You know, Esther, she told you often enough. You just don't like to listen.'

Esther flinched. She'd no idea her mother had told Gladys quite so much. Tears swilled in her eyes. Not only had her father let her mother down, now she had too.

'But she's defaulted on her payments now! She's going to lose everything.'

She was already upset but now she was completely and utterly overwhelmed. She didn't know how they could possibly find any way out of this. The repairs to the house would require another mortgage—and could you even get a re-mortgage on a house that was fire damaged?

As for the contents—the entire kitchen would need to replaced, and the roof. That was before they even thought about the decor. Esther put her head in her hands. She had no idea what to do next. This was so much worse than she'd first imagined.

'Who's going to lose everything?' Harry's voice came from the doorway and both heads snapped around to his.

'Maybe I should leave you both alone,' said Gladys quickly, standing up to leave.

'No,' said Harry as he crossed the room and held his hand out to Esther. 'You've been so good already.' He looked down at Esther. 'Why don't we get some fresh air?'

Esther's head was swimming. She couldn't even begin to think about what all this meant. But Harry was right. She'd imposed on Gladys long enough. She didn't want to have a complete breakdown in front of the poor woman. Fresh air wouldn't help, but it would give her a bit of space.

She gave a reluctant nod and stood up, putting her hand in Harry's. 'We'll walk to the hospital. It will be visiting time soon and I want to see how she's doing.' She glanced back to Gladys. 'Please don't tell anyone about this. Let me see if there's anything else I can do.'

Gladys gave a thoughtful nod and left them to walk outside.

Esther was trying her best to hold it together. She got as far as the end of the street, where Harry seemed to know to lead her over to the empty children's swing park.

He sat her down on one of the swings and put his hands on her shoulders. 'Tell me what's happened.'

She couldn't stop crying. 'I didn't send her enough money. She missed her insurance payments. She had no insurance. I have no idea how we can fix the house.' By the end her words barely came out at all and Harry just pulled her towards him, letting her sob. 'This is all my fault.'

Part of him twisted inside. When he'd first met Esther she'd worked every hour on the planet. He'd been the one to encourage her to take some time off. He'd been the one to persuade her to spend one day a week with him. The nights just hadn't been enough for him. He'd wanted more. He'd wanted every day. Look what his actions had caused. A horrible sick feeling rose in his stomach. He couldn't let her think this was her fault. Not for a second.

He bent down and pushed back the hair that had stuck to her face. 'Esther, we can sort this.'

'How?' Her eyes were bright with tears.

He pulled a set of keys from his pocket. 'I didn't go for coffee. I called a letting agency and picked up some keys to a house, a few streets over. Your mum can move in straight away until things get sorted.'

She stared at the silver keys in amazement. 'You did what? But you didn't know anything.'

'But I'd seen the house. I knew she couldn't go back there tonight. And I know that if she's anything like her daughter, she won't want to stay with someone else and impose.'

Esther took a few deep breaths. Her brain had been whirling so much she hadn't even considered tonight. 'But—'

'We can all stay there. The letting agent was in the area and was able to show me around. It's clean, tidy and furnished. We can go and get some bedsheets and some towels before we collect your mum from the hospital.'

'But… I need to pay you… How much was this?'

'Nothing,' came the quick reply.

'No.' She shook her head firmly. 'No way.'

But Harry turned to her with an equally determined look. 'Esther, if you hadn't been with me, if I hadn't *persuaded* you to take some time off, you would still have been able to send the money to your mother that she needed.' He put his hand on his chest. 'This is my fault. Not yours. And I'm so, so sorry.'

Her nose wrinkled. 'How can you think this is your fault?'

He held out his hands. 'Because I wanted you. I wanted all of you. I wanted all your time and all your attention. Being around you has been special for me. You've opened my eyes to so many things. You've brought fun into my life—something I never really thought I might deserve.' He paused for a second. 'And the relationship you have with your mum? Made me ask myself questions about how things turned out with my dad. Ones that I hadn't wanted to give myself the time to examine, because I wouldn't like the answers.'

She shook her head. 'But I've let her down, Harry. I've painted you a rosy picture of my life. And I do have a great relationship with my mum. I love her. I'd do anything for her. But my dad…' She let her voice trail for a second. 'Things weren't perfect. He was a drifter. A dreamer. And every time he jumped from one job to the next, he made life harder for my mum. He let her down. And I think I've done that too.'

'What?'

She sniffed and took a deep breath to stop the words from getting stuck in her throat. 'She kept telling me not to work too hard. She kept telling me to get the work/life balance right. But I kept being single-minded. I kept wanting to work too hard, even though my body was telling me to stop.' Her eyes locked with his. 'Then I met you, Harry. I started to realise what fun was. And I kept telling myself this was a fling. A temporary thing. That it would go nowhere. But deep down, my heart wasn't listening. It was jumping in, feet first. Even though my brain knows I can't do this to myself. I can't fall for a guy who isn't around. I've already been hurt by that man. My father.' She whispered, 'I'm sorry, Harry. I should have stopped this before it started.'

His eyes went wide. She half expected him to argue back with her, to fight with her. But he surprised her by taking a deep breath and sitting down on the swing next to her, interlocking his fingers with hers. It took him a few minutes to start speaking. 'I thought when I came up here today, I just had to explain about the photo. I thought once you realised there was nothing in it, we could be fine.'

Esther froze. 'And now you think we can't?'

It didn't matter that she'd realised inside that she had to stay in Scotland. That it was likely there was no way to keep their relationship afloat. Now that he might be saying it back, every part of her body wanted to protest. To grab him and hold him tight again. To tell him that there had to be a way.

'We're so different,' he said sadly.

'You're right, we are so different,' she agreed. 'And if I was feeling really brave I would tell you that fairy tales aren't real. Not for people like me.'

He looked over at her with wounded eyes. 'So, why does it feel like—no matter what else has gone on—the only thing that really matters to me is you?' He ran his other hand through his hair and shook his head. 'I don't even deserve you, Esther. I'm not good enough for you. You've got a big heart. You're easy to love, and I can't promise you that I can be the same.'

'Why on earth would you think you're not good enough for me?'

His head fell. 'Because you know how to live life. Love. You've lived it every day of your life. You embrace it. You and your mum wouldn't know any other way to be.' He shook his head.

'My experience of love has been very different to yours. Non-existent even. How can I ever be what you need me to be?'

She could almost feel something tear at her heart muscles. She loved this guy. She loved him so much it could physically hurt if she let it. And here he was, thinking he wasn't good enough for her. Thinking he didn't have enough love to offer because of the messages he'd been left with by his mum and dad.

She tilted her head to the side. 'But everyone's got to start somewhere, Harry. Nature, or nurture? We could argue for both. I would say that every day of your life you've learned to love something. Whether it was a person, or a thing, a pet, a food, a moment.' She held up her hands. 'A sight, a sound, a taste. All of them build the person that you are, and from where I'm sitting—' she gave him a half-smile '—you don't look too bad.'

He smiled and shook his head, his voice barely a whisper. 'I'm going to tell you something I've never told anyone. When I heard that my father was dead, part of me was relieved to be free of the storm clouds that felt as if they constantly hung over my head. But part of me—' his voice trembled a little '—was still that five-year-old little kid, wondering what on earth he could do to make his mum and dad love him the way that other families did. It seemed like something was wrong with me. And I wanted to be... I wanted to be enough.' He reached over and touched her cheek. 'You were the first person that made me think I might be good enough. Good enough to love. You don't care about the duke stuff. You don't care about the surgeon stuff. And I too thought this would just be fun. Just be a fling. But, Esther—' he put his hand to his chest '—I can't be that person. I can't be the person that moves around. I've spent so long looking for love that now that I've found it, I don't ever want to let it go. I want to be enough. I want to be more than enough for you. I've never wanted anything more. I don't want to live this life without you.'

He was looking right at her, and she could feel the question in the air.

Her hand was trembling as she reached up and ran her fingers through his hair. 'Harry, what you told me about your father? That you'd never told anyone else? It makes my heart break for that five-year-old boy. It takes a lot to admit that you still wanted that connection—after everything that happened. That no matter how much he'd hurt you, you still wished for something different.'

He shook his head and closed his eyes. 'Five minutes. A five-minute conversation to see if he would ever have changed his mind. Regretted how things had been. But it wasn't to be. And I'll always have to wonder.'

She pressed her hands on either side of his head. 'But you don't have to wonder. Because I can tell you. You're worthy of love, Harry. I love you so much I think my heart might burst. I have never, ever loved anyone the way that I love you, and I never, ever will. Because you have my heart, Harry Beaumont. You have all of it.'

Now she saw tears swimming in his eyes as he bent his head towards hers.

She held her breath. 'Everything's such a mix-up right now. I have so much work to do here. To help my mum, to get back on our feet.'

'Is that a no?' he asked in a quiet voice.

'No. It's not.' She said it so quickly it surprised even herself. It was completely instinctual and straight from the heart.

He stood up and pulled her towards him. 'Tell me what you want, Esther. Tell me what you need.'

Here it was. Everything she'd ever wanted.

That was the laugh. She'd never even known she wanted this. She'd never even dared to dream she would be the Cinderella girl. It hadn't even occurred to her—not for a second. Her dreams had always been about earning money and living independently, and part of her was still that girl.

'I need some time,' she breathed. 'I need some time to sort things out.' The keys were clenched in her hand. 'These are a godsend. Thank you. It means my mum can have a roof over her head until I try and see if I can sort the insurance out.'

'Or you could let me sort the insurance out.'

She pressed her lips together and looked up at him with her blue eyes. Her heart was swelling in her chest as if it would burst. 'If I said yes, I wouldn't be me. And my heart would be sad forever.'

His face broke into a wide smile and he slid his fingers through her hair. 'I wouldn't love you any other way.' He closed his eyes for a second and gave a slow nod. 'How about, if you didn't say yes. How about, if something just happened that allowed your mother to rebuild her house?'

Her hands were on his arms now. He was treading so carefully, respecting her space, but still trying to help.

She let out a half-laugh. 'What on earth could happen?'

'A lottery ticket. A windfall. A forgotten pension of your father's. An old insurance policy that everyone had misplaced and now secretly pays out.'

She held her breath. He knew her pride would

never let her accept direct money from him. He guessed her mother would be exactly the same. Now, he was giving her a get-out clause. A way that she could sort things for her mother, with a little help from Harry.

'Where did I find you?' she whispered, her hand reaching up to thread through his hair.

He was doing this for her. To let her save face. To let her pride stay intact. To stop her feeling as if everything was outside of her control, and that everything was hopeless.

He leaned forward and murmured in her ear. 'You found me in a scary place with tiny babies. It's where I'm most at home—and where I think that you're most at home too.'

Tears brimmed in her eyes. She'd started this day thinking the man she loved had betrayed her, and she'd have to pack up and leave the job she loved in London to help out her mum.

Now, he was right by her side and offering her an opportunity to stay, with both him and the job she loved.

'I have something else to tell you,' he said quietly. 'And I hope it's what you want to hear.' He tightened his arms a little around her. 'I've said yes to something else.'

'What?'

He breathed slowly. 'I've said yes to a permanent position at the Queen Victoria with my own team. I said yes because I've found the place I want to be home for me. And that's with you. I'll help you sort things with your mum. Because you don't need to do this on your own. You don't need to carry the load on your own. I'm right here, Esther. And I plan on staying.'

She leaned back but stayed in his arms. 'Harry?'

He put a gentle finger to her lips. 'I know there are a hundred questions. Maybe even a thousand what-ifs. But let's start with the most important one. I love you, Esther. Whether things are good or bad, I want to be by your side. I can't imagine loving anyone else the way that I love you.'

Nerves made her interrupt. 'Is that a question?'

He smiled. 'I know it's soon. I know you might think I'm crazy, but I guess now I've found somebody to love, I want to tell the world.' His words were soft, quiet and straight from the heart. 'So, after we've sorted everything for your mum, how do you feel about making things more permanent between us? Will you move in with me, Esther?' His gaze fixed on hers. 'Will you marry me?'

Every part of her body rejoiced. 'You want to get married?' She laughed.

'Yes.' He nodded. Then he looked at her. 'Wait, why are you laughing?'

Esther didn't stop. 'You think someone like me should be the Duchess of Montrose?'

He picked her up and spun her around. 'I think someone like you should be *exactly* the Duchess of Montrose.' He lowered her slowly to the ground, letting their bodies brush against one another. 'What can I say? Scottish.' He smiled. 'At least you'll be the genuine article.'

She wound her arms around his neck. 'Oh, so was it me you wanted, or was it any old Scottish girl?'

His lips lowered towards hers. 'Don't doubt for a second, it was definitely you.' Then he stopped, as if he'd just realised something. 'Hey? Was that a yes?'

She nodded. 'That was definitely a yes,' she murmured as her lips touched his.

CHAPTER TWELVE

'HE'S SUCH A nice young man,' sighed Esther's mum from her prime position on the sofa. She hadn't taken her eyes off him since they'd been introduced in the hospital and Harry had put all the arrangements in place to get her back to her new temporary home.

She ran her hand along the yellow sofa. 'This place is so nice. It was lucky you were able to get it at such short notice.' She lifted her chin and looked out of the window. From here she could see right along the coastline to Leith. 'I've never had a sea view,' she murmured.

'Do you like it?' asked Esther curiously.

'Of course I like it.' Her mother smiled. 'It's my dream house.'

Harry walked up behind Esther with some papers in his hand. 'Then it's lucky you don't have to move out.'

Esther blinked. 'What?'

Harry gave her a quick glance, then smiled

at her mother. 'This house was up for rent, with the chance to buy. With the insurance money to fix your home, once that's done, you could sell your other place and move permanently here if you like.'

Esther reached behind her and grabbed his hand. She knew exactly what he was doing. There was no insurance money, but they'd both agreed not to tell her mother that.

'But isn't this place much more expensive than my house?'

Of course it was. But Harry spoke smoothly. 'This is a flat. Not a house. Esther can take care of things regarding the sale and purchase, but if you like this place best, there's no reason you couldn't have it.' He bent down next to her head and glanced out the window. 'You're right, the sea view is nice.'

Now he was bending things a little further. Letting her mum feel as if all of this was being done within her own budget.

Her mum pulled the blanket up to her chest and gave Esther a nervous glance. 'You know, I wouldn't need to worry about the garden, and there's a security entrance here, and a lift.' She ran her hand back along the sofa. 'And everything is just so new.' Esther could almost see her mum's heart jump. 'And there's room enough for you and Harry to stay too when you visit.'

Oh dear. For about the tenth time in twenty-four hours, tears threatened to spill. But these were happy tears. Esther sat on the sofa next to her mum and gave her a giant hug. The lines on her face didn't seem quite so deep, and she had a little colour back in her cheeks. 'Leave it with me, and Harry,' she added as she shot him a smile. 'We'll take care of everything for you.'

He gave a nod and knelt down in front of them. 'There is one final thing,' he said, reaching into his back pocket.

Esther caught her breath at the sight of the small black velvet box. When on earth had he had time to go shopping for that?

It flipped open, showing one of the biggest emeralds she'd ever seen, with a diamond set on either side. 'Family heirloom,' he said. 'It belonged to the last duchess who had Scottish blood in her veins, my great-great-grandmother, so I thought it might be fitting.'

He pulled it from the box. 'Esther McDonald. You've brought light and life and joy into my life and I hope to do the same to yours. Now, and always. Will you do me the pleasure of becoming my wife?'

She couldn't speak at first, just gave a nod as she held out a trembling hand and let Harry slip the giant ring on her finger.

Her mother let out a squeal and started clapping as Harry picked her up and spun her round and round and round.

As he set her back down he whispered in her ear. 'So, Duchess of Montrose, what will be your first wish?'

Her eyes gleamed. 'That? Oh, that's definitely for later, and for just you, and me,' she said as she kissed him once again.

* * * * *